Marked Wolf

Iron Beast Pack Book One

Angelica Aquiles

MARKED WOLF

Copyright © 2022 by Angelica Aquiles

This is a work of fiction. Names, characters, places, brands, media, and incidents are either the products of the author's imagination or are used fictitiously.

Copy/Line Editing: Heather Fox at Fox Proof Editing

Cover Design: Francesca Michelon at MerryBookRound

Formatting by: The Nutty Formatter

To my husband and my kids letting me spend too much time on the computer. Love you guys!

WARNING

Please be aware that this book contains cheating NOT from her Harem!

This book contains adult content and mature language. It is intended for readers 18+. Please note this is a Why Choose Romance which means Kat will have multiple love interests.

Enjoy!

Chapter 1

Kat

I t's the middle of a workday, and my husband's favorite Armani suit rests in a heap in the hallway, the first indication that my relaxing day would be anything but that. I set my purse and the takeout bags on the foyer table, moving toward the pile of discarded clothes, but when I see a pair of women's pumps sitting neatly outside our bedroom door, my heart stalls. There's a lace thong lying next to Theo's suit and an expensive pencil skirt that's been pulled inside out in a hurry. I want to turn around now and pretend this isn't happening, but I push the door open in a haze of fear and nausea. My body trembles from anger and disappointment as tears run down my face.

Theo's arms are strained as he holds the headboard tightly. The loose nails creak and the bed looks as if it's about to fall apart. I guess that answers the question of why it's been so wobbly lately. But according to him, *"nothing is wrong with it."*

Beads of sweat run down his back as he thrusts his dick back and forth uncontrollably with so much heat and passion

The coffee from this morning roils in my belly. Thankfully, I had nothing to eat, or it would be all over the floor right now.

He's grunting loudly, ready to find his release, and though I haven't heard him make these sounds in a long time, I can tell he's about to finish.

The woman underneath him lets out a fake as hell moan, almost as if she knows she has an audience and is trying to put on a show. I watch her face contort as she cries out, her fingers digging into my favorite silk pillowcase beneath her head. He trusts a few more times before he groans and leans into her, his head falling as he finishes inside her.

My body sags against the doorframe, unable to stand on my own or move from this spot. I'm heartbroken, sick to my stomach, absolutely wrecked by what's in front of me.

My mind doesn't want to believe it, but I'm catching him right in the act.

Sixteen years together…thrown away for five minutes inside some blonde bimbo. We had a beautiful life; we built our house from the ground up and have two amazing children that are nearly grown. I spent a lifetime playing the good housewife while he opened his own practice and built his career as the best family law attorney in the city. I was so proud of him.

He turns around to face me as though he can feel someone staring at the back of his head. If looks could kill, he'd be dead now, but fortunately for him, they don't.

"Fuck, you're home early." His raven hair sticks to his sweaty forehead as he turns his cold black eyes to me with no emotion. He's surprised to see me, but there's no remorse on his face as he scans the room quickly for something to cover himself with. The man that's slept naked next to me for all these years is embarrassed to be undressed in front of me. How did we get here? This explains why he won't touch me anymore. I should have known something like this was going on. I should have put the pieces together, but I never wanted to believe he was capable of something like this. I wanted to believe he still loved me.

When he finds his boxers on the floor, he swiftly picks them up and tries to get dressed. I almost forgot how fit he is underneath his suits. The woman lying in my bed rises to her elbows and I realize that I know her. Krissy, his twenty-five-year-old assistant, has clearly been working overtime lately. As she climbs from my side of the bed, she looks over me judgmentally, and I can't help the sudden urge I feel to cover my fully dressed body.

I know I shouldn't compare the two of us, but she looks so much better than I do. I'm surprised to find she has tattoos because Theo never wanted me to get any. He's always been against them. The only one I have is a small heart right below the corner of my eye. I cross my arms trying not to cower from her harsh stare. I don't know why she's judging me— she's the homewrecker. What makes me the most uncomfortable is the way she acts like she fits in perfectly and I am the one intruding.

She takes her time finding clothes, and I can't help but notice how fit her body is. I can tell she hasn't had kids by her slim build and perky boobs. No matter how much I exercise or how healthy I eat, my body won't ever look the way it did before kids. I've always been completely fine with that. My stretch marks and curves were worth it because I love my kids more than anything.

There's a glint in her eye while she smirks, almost like she's won a battle I didn't know I was fighting. Tears threaten to well up in my eyes, but I won't give her the satisfaction of seeing me at my most vulnerable.

He walks up to me, more annoyed by getting caught than

sorry for what he's done. How long has he been doing this? Has he had many women or is Krissy the only one?

My heart plummets as he sails past me without a word, and Krissy bounces behind him shamelessly. All the love I have for this man, and he throws it away without an ounce of remorse. My arms shake as I wrap them across my chest tightly, resisting the urge to reach out and grab Krissy by her bottle-blonde hair and throw her ass outside.

He opens the door to let her out, and to my utter shock, she stands on her toes to give him a kiss on the cheek. "Bye babe," she says as if my husband is her boyfriend. My mouth hangs open in shock. I'm speechless. The realization hits me, this has been going on for a while.

When he closes the door, I start shouting. "So I'm only going to ask you once." Putting my hand on my hip, I raise one of my eyebrows, giving him my fiercest look and standing as tall as my five-foot frame allows. "How long have you been fucking your assistant?" I blurt out in the most enraged tone I can muster. I didn't know I had that in me, but just looking at his indifferent face brings out my inner animal.

My whole body shakes impatiently waiting for a response, but I don't have to wait long. "We…" he points between us, "just don't work out anymore."

There's no sympathy in his words or sorrow in his eyes. My stomach churns with the realization of what's about to happen. This is not something that has ever crossed my mind. I know we've been busy and distant, but I really thought he was happy.

"You're leaving my ass because you think we don't work out together anymore? So, that piece of ass on the side has nothing to do with it?" I scoff.

We've got a sixteen-year-old and a fifteen-year-old and I haven't worked outside of the home since they were babies.

Who is going to want to hire a grown-ass woman that has been out of the workforce this long? I'm livid with him, but more than that, I'm angry with myself.

"Look, we both know this is long overdue. I'll give you the week to figure out where you and the kids are going to go." His harsh words fill me with a whole new reason to panic. I have nowhere to go, no family to take us in. I spent my childhood bouncing around in foster homes after my parents were deported back to Nicaragua, a small country in central America. I was too little to remember them, and the foster families I was placed with never wanted more than the government check attached to me.

I clench my shaking fists at my sides. I've never wanted to hit someone so much in my life. I'm thankful that the kids aren't home from school yet and they can't hear our bickering, but I'm sure the whole nosey neighborhood has their ears close to their doors.

It's Monday, he can't expect me to be out of the house by Friday. "What about our kids? They need a place to stay. I need more time," I plead with him, even if it makes me look weak. Five days to find a place seems impossible with no income and no family to help. We're going to end up on the streets and I can't let that happen.

"I don't even know if those kids are mine." My vision changes and all I see is red.

"What do you mean you don't know if these are your kids?" I say so silently that I see his body twitch slightly in fear. His arrogance is almost completely gone. He just realized he said the wrong thing. Good. No one ever fucking messes with my kids, not even their own father.

I pull one chancla from my foot and throw it over my head. He tries to duck but it still hits him in the forehead. I grab the other one from my foot and do it again. He tries to cover his face but he's too slow and it knocks him in the nose. I let myself smile slightly at the victory. "You're the only one I've fucked, Theo. I never cheated on you. I've always been a faithful little housewife, and for what?" I shout again. "For you to leave me for another woman." I probably sound like a maniac to anyone listening into our conversation, but I'm so hurt that I don't care.

"I can't do this anymore," he says, turning toward our bedroom. "I'm not coming back here until you and the kids leave."

I walk into the room after him, watching to see what he does next. He grabs a suitcase from the walk-in closet and pulls some of his suits from the rack.

"I'll have my assistant draw up the divorce paperwork when I get to work in the morning. You'll probably need a good fucking lawyer if you think you're taking me for half of anything. I could probably recommend a colleague or two that takes on a few pro bono cases a month, but really, we'd just be going through the motions, wouldn't we? You know there's no family lawyer in this state that can work the system the way that I can."

An evil smile stretches over his handsome face as he reaches the front door.

"What about the kids?" Tears fill my eyes again as he turns to me and shakes his head.

"You're not getting a fucking cent from me for your kids, not anymore." He slams the door in my face before I can beg him to reconsider, and my whole world crumbles at my feet.

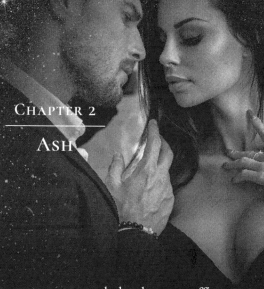

CHAPTER 2

ASH

I'm shuffling the papers on my desk when my office door slams open suddenly. Amara stands before me panting for air, her face slick with sweat and her messy hair sticking up in every direction. "What is it?" I ask, seeing the urgency on her face as she falls into the chair in front of my desk with a huff. She's breathing like she ran the two miles between her house and mine.

"I'm not sure. This caught me by surprise and I had to get here as soon as it happened." She rubs her eyes with the heels of her hands as if she just woke up, and I lean in closer to wait for her explanation.

Amara doesn't look any older than twenty-six, but she's the oldest witch in her coven and the leader. "What happened?" I press, anxious for details.

"My ancestors whispered in my ear, telling me that all four of you need to be at the diner by six tonight."

"Diner? What are you talking about?"

"You and your brothers." She's referring to my best friends, the other three Alpha's that make up the Iron Beast Pack. "You need to retrieve a girl and bring her here."

"Why would we risk our time finding a girl we've never met and play babysitter? We don't do that shit."

"Ash, I don't think you have a choice." She bites her lip, probably afraid I'm going to lash out at her demands. Maybe I would have, but I'm starting to get this strange feeling in the pit of my stomach.

"What else did they say?" The unease is growing and I don't like it.

"To let you know that this is urgent, and if you choose to ignore this, there will be consequences." There's a pain growing in the back of my head.

"What is her name?" I ask, knowing I have no choice but to follow through with the task.

"Katarina, but she goes by Kat." The wolf inside me perks up when I hear the girl's name.

I test the way her nickname sounds a couple of times. Nah, I think I'll call her Katarina. I love the way her full name rolls off my tongue.

"She also has two kids, a fifteen and sixteen-year-old." Well, this should be fun. "You can't let the council find her, Ash. Promise me that you won't." She gives me a pointed stare. I can see it in her gray eyes, she's putting all her trust in me.

She hands me a piece of paper and I open it. It has the address to a place that I've never been before. Sofie's Diner.

"We're so close to tracking that witch, Amara. I can feel it." She sighs tirelessly. She knows what this means to us and the rest of her people.

"Maybe we'll get another opportunity," she says sadly. I promised her as much as my brothers that we will never give up.

"Are you sure this girl Katarina is more important?" I try

again, already knowing the answer but needing a confirmation one last time.

"Don't question me," she says as if I just insulted her. She grabs her long red hair and ties it up in a ponytail before trying another approach. "All I know is that she's important," she says softly, staring off into space for a second. I wonder if her ancestors are talking to her right now. She looks troubled, which makes me a little queasy.

We often look to Amara for advice and guidance, and it gnaws on her that she doesn't know much about our situation.

I sit back wondering what mess I've just signed us up for. We have other things to worry about and I really don't want to waste my time driving three hours when we've got better things going on. But I do as she says because she wouldn't have told me about this unless it's serious.

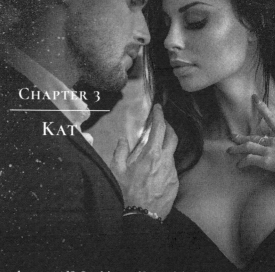

CHAPTER 3

KAT

W hat just happened? Is this real? I wish it had been a horrible nightmare, but I know better.

I slam my back against the door and slide all the way down, sobbing into my hands. My heart hurts for myself, but more than that, for my kids. Did he really deny they were his? What kind of father does that? Oh right, Theo does. That piece of shit human being.

What the fuck am I going to do now? We got married at eighteen. He got me pregnant at sixteen with our first child and shortly after, I got pregnant again at seventeen.

I haven't worked in so long I don't think anyone would hire me. My plan was to go back to school once he opened his own practice and the kids were older, but he always told me not to worry about it. He said he'd take care of us, and I was dumb enough to believe him. I shake my head softly. I should have known better.

I always took care of myself, but it was nice when Theo finally came along as my knight to spare me from my terrible life. I saw him as my savior, the person who could take me out of my horrible upbringing. He was the light to my darkness, the person sent to finally get me out of the hell I lived in.

But instead, he set me up to fail or…maybe I failed myself. Now I have nothing to my name. Everything is under his, the mortgage, the cars. He always told me that it just made life easier to have one owner, and like a dumbass, I agreed thinking he'd always have my best interest at heart.

Once I can manage to hold back my tears, I unload the takeout bags on the dining room table for the kids and call my best friend, Jess. Just like me, she had absolutely nothing growing up. She was so happy when I told her about Theo, but when she finally met him, she said he was a devil in disguise. She pleaded with me not to be with him, but by then it was too late. I was already pregnant.

It goes straight to voicemail. Debating whether to leave a message, I decide not to, but I open my mouth and words fall from my lips without permission. "Jess, he left me." I begin crying again. "He had another girl on the side." I quickly hang up the phone because I'd rather not pour my heart out to her voicemail. It's only going to make her more frantic.

I walk into the office and start up the computer. How do I look for a place to live with no money? It's not like I can ask my old foster family to help me. They haven't contacted me even once after all these years. They're probably still collecting paychecks from other kids.

I was sixteen when I met Theo, and he was sixteen, about to enter law school the following year. At the time, I was waitressing to save up money for college because there was no one to help me besides myself.

Theo would come in every day and make sure he sat at one of my tables. He was always really kind.

He told me that he wanted to take me out on a date. I was hesitant at first because I had big dreams and didn't want to lose my focus. I was going to be free in two years and then my life would be mine. I wouldn't have to go to random homes where the men always looked at me like I was a piece of meat, and the woman spent my monthly check on drugs and alcohol.

Moving from house to house, I never had friends. I was always a loner. So when Theo approached me, I was skeptical. Jess was in the last house I stayed in when I turned fifteen. She was my age and we got along well. We had the same struggles, and because of our similarities, our bond grew. We were all each other had.

Theo asked me out a few times before I finally gave in. He took me to eat at a fancy restaurant and I was smitten. He wasn't rich, but because he was an only child, he got everything he wanted. He bought me nice things I could never afford on my own.

When he found out I was pregnant, he didn't look thrilled about being a dad. I thought it was because he was scared like me. I could barely take care of myself and then I was supposed to take care of a baby. But once she was born, all I could think about was being the best mom to her.

Then I got pregnant again and it was the same thing. He didn't show any emotion and he got a vasectomy so we wouldn't have any more kids.

I was so happy with my two kids that I didn't think about it much until now. He never really wanted children. When he started coming home later and later, I thought it was because he had a lot of work to do, but maybe I was wrong. He might have been cheating on me this whole time and just finally let me go because he found someone worth fighting for.

I swallow through a thick lump in my throat, focusing back on the computer. I'm not even sure how to look for a place. *Craigslist?*

I look through some of the listings, wondering how I'm going to pay for a place to stay with my kids. I go through the scenarios of working a minimum wage job, and even if I worked, I wouldn't be able to afford it. I'd have to work three jobs to barely survive. I rub my eyes, stressing out about the time limit he's given me.

I'm startled when the front door opens and I close the browser quickly. I walk back into the living room just as my kids are walking in.

I try to keep a brave face so they won't see what's going on. "Dinner is ready. Food is sitting on the table. You guys eat and I'll be right out." I'm surprised by how calm my voice sounds when I still feel like crying.

Ezra, my fifteen-year-old, has Theo's dark hair and eyes with my honey kissed skin. He's the first through the door, followed by Ava, my sixteen-year-old, and from what I've been told, she's the spitting image of me. Except she has wavy hair and mine is straight.

They stare at me like I'm crazy, but what's new? They've looked at me that way since they started their teens.

My phone rings and I glance down, seeing that it's my best friend Jess. I quickly go into my room and shut the door. I don't want the kids to see me tearing up right now. "Katarina." She only uses my full name if she's serious, normally she calls me Kat like everyone else. "What happened?" Worry with a hint of anger laces her voice.

"He left me." I try to keep my composure before tears start to spill again. I'm such a mess, but I've been betrayed by my partner.

"What the fuck!" she shouts into the line in irritation, but I know it's not directed at me. She always thought he wasn't good enough, and though she wanted to be wrong, she never missed an opportunity to tell me that I could do better.

"Do you have time to meet me for dinner? We can talk about it there and you can let it all out hon." She's talking about the local place we meet up for breakfast sometimes.

That's probably a good idea. I need to get out of this house, even if it's for a little bit. Maybe I'll ask if we can stay with her for a little while until I get some funds to rent a place of my own.

"Yeah, okay. Is an hour good?" I ask, holding my phone a little too tightly.

"Perfect. I should be out of work by then. See you soon." I sigh in relief just for a small moment. She is my anchor.

"Thanks girl." I hang up the phone while looking in the mirror. I take deep breaths trying to compose myself and to keep the tears from running down my face, but there is nothing I can do. No matter how much I try to hold it together, they keep falling. My light brown eyes look hollow and pained. My full lips are swollen and cracked with blood from all the biting I've been doing. There's no way to hide that I've been crying, so I smooth the wisps of dark hair that brush against my shoulders and turn to go back into the kitchen.

I sit at the end of the table across from the kids, trying not to look at the empty seat where their father should be. "How was school?" I try to act like it's just an ordinary day. I know that I have to tell them sooner rather than later, but I'm not ready to have that conversation yet.

"Boring," Ezra says, picking at his food. He's always been a picky eater. He usually won't finish the meals I buy or make.

"It was okay. I've got a test to study for," Ava says, focusing more on her food than our conversation.

At her age, I was pregnant with her, so there's always that hint of worry that gnaws on me. She hasn't shown much interest in boys, but she could easily be hiding it from me.

There's not much conversation after that. We eat silently as I watch the kids pick the meat off their salads. I can practically hear Theo's usual scolding about being wasteful and picky.

They haven't asked about their dad yet since they are used to him 'working' long hours lately. I know it'll come, and I'm not prepared for it. Ezra and Ava rinse their plates and disappear into their rooms. Not once did they comment on my blotchy face. I don't think they even noticed and I'm so grateful for that.

Cleaning up the rest of the dishes, I decide to get ready, and by getting ready I mean dabbing my cheeks from the tears that are still freely falling.

I knock softly on their doors and they both come out. "I'm meeting Jess at the diner. I'm leaving now." I look away from them so that they won't see me crying. I'm not ready for that conversation yet.

"Okay. Bye, Mom." Ezra closes the door and goes back to what he was doing.

"See you later." Ava follows and closes her door.

Okay, not much love from those two. *Teenagers.*

Grabbing my coat from the rack, I reach for my keys, but they're not there. I remember hanging them before walking into the house, but now they're gone. Did he take the keys? I check my oversized purse in case I might have thrown them in there by accident, but they're not there.

The realization hits me. "Shit, I have no car," I say out loud. It looks like I'll have to walk instead. I think about calling Jessica for a ride, but maybe being outside and taking in some fresh air will do me some good. I grab a small pocket knife in case I come across any weirdos since it will be dark soon. I'll have to make sure to ask Jess for a ride back home. The last thing that I need is to get kidnapped.

I make my way out of the house and down the driveway, giving my car one last longing look and letting out a sigh.

There are rows of houses lined up like mine, all with perfectly groomed lawns. I always dreamed of living in a neighborhood like this one, where my kids could play outside with other kids. I never had that experience growing up, and I've always wanted more for them. But now, I feel like I've failed.

It's getting darker and chillier than I would have thought. I keep my hand in my pocket with my fingers gripping my knife in case anything happens. I should have just called Jessica to come pick me up.

CHAPTER 4

KAT

I t's clear out, making the full moon bright this evening.
Normally the night sky would be overshadowed by dark
clouds. I've always hated the cold and wanted to move
somewhere warmer. But Theo loves Washington, so we
stayed.

I reminisce on one of the few trips we took. I begged him
to go to Hawaii and he finally took me. The weather was
gorgeous, and the beaches were clear with pretty blues and
greens surrounding the island. I had never seen a beach
before then. I try to remember the beautiful scenery and the
warmth as I make my way down the freezing path. Yep, I'm
regretting this idea.

I walk four blocks and go through an alley behind a
couple of restaurants trying to get to Sofie's Diner faster.
Figured I'd take a shortcut, even if it does look kind of
sketchy. I want to be there as soon as I can just to make it out
of the cold. I underestimated how chilly it was going to be.
I'm shivering from head to toe. I wrap my coat tighter like it's
going to somehow add another layer of warmth, but it doesn't

help any. I'm glad I found gloves in one of the pockets or else my fingers would be frostbitten.

I've never gone for a walk at night outside of walking to and from my car. I think that one of the things I might need to prioritize is getting a vehicle. There is no way I can make my way places in this gruesome weather.

I keep walking until the hairs on the back of my neck stand to attention as if I'm being watched. I look around frantically trying to see who's following me when I immediately spot a bigger than normal sized dog. I stand still, barely breathing, not wanting to attract the animal's attention as he growls in my direction.

My heartbeat becomes erratic, and I clutch my purse for dear life like it's going to somehow protect me. A bead of cold sweat trickles down my forehead as the dog studies my body posture. It seems to be very aware of how nervous I am, or maybe I smell like fear.

Terrified of getting eaten, I don't want to make any sudden movements, but it's looking at me like I'm dinner. My body is paralyzed in fear. *Do dogs eat humans? God, I hope not.*

After what feels like an eternity, the big dog comes charging straight at me aggressively with its nostrils flaring. My eyes widen and my pulse races. In a panic, I look around for a place to run and hide but can't find a good spot.

This fucking day just keeps getting better.

I tell my body to move, but my head and limbs aren't working together. Come on, come on, I try to give myself a pep talk. When my body finally moves, it feels heavy, like bricks are attached to my legs. I try to hide behind the nearest dumpster outside one of the restaurants, knowing it won't do anything, but right now, it gives me a sense of security.

With shaky hands, I pull my knife from my coat pocket,

hoping that I won't need to use it on that big motherfucker. Despite how aggressive the dog is, I'd feel bad about hurting it. But if it's between me or him then I'll choose me. I don't know if that makes me selfish, maybe it does, but I have my kids to think about. Anything for them, even if I have to kill an animal and feel guilty later.

I flip the lever open and the silver point shines against the full moon. I wait for it to come to me. Everything out here seems to be quiet except for my breathing and the loud pounding going off in my chest. If that four-legged animal doesn't kill me, my heart will for sure.

After waiting around for five minutes, or at least it feels that long, I get the courage to walk slowly to the edge of the bin, surprised to find the dog is nowhere in sight. It probably got tired of waiting for me. I try to calm my breathing before I make a run for it. I'm so close to the diner, all I need to do is make it to the other side of the street.

As soon as I take the first step, I hear a snarl right behind me. My body trembles violently. I turn my head very slowly, and all I can see is its mouth with saliva dripping from it. Realizing that this is no big dog at all…oh God, I think I'm about to puke. All I know is that I need to get out of here before it attacks me. I try to move again when it leaps in midair, pushing my whole body to the ground. The small knife flies from my hand into the darkness. Fuck.

I try to push the dog off me while it snaps its jaws, showing me those sharp teeth.

When it reaches down to my neck, my life flashes before my eyes. I'm going to die. I shut my eyes tightly knowing that these are my last few moments before I'm taken from this world.

I'm saddened by the fact that Theo won't take care of the kids and they'll probably end up separated in the foster care system just like me. He never wanted them. I just didn't realize that until today. My cheeks are wet with tears.

For my kids, I have to give it one last try. I refuse to leave them to that fate. I push back with the last bit of energy that I have. Big jaws keep trying to bite me, but the dog doesn't quite reach my neck…yet.

My arms shake as I curl my fingers into the animal's thick fur and push his head away from me. My strength is wavering, and I can no longer sustain this position. Exhaustion slowly takes over as the adrenaline drains from my body.

As much as I want to fight, there's no way I can hold this animal off. It's too heavy. It probably weighs more than two hundred pounds.

My arms finally buckle under the beast's weight and a sob tears from my throat as my hands fall limply over my chest.

I watch with wide eyes as its jaw opens, showing its razor-sharp canines. It brings one giant paw up and pushes my face to the side, exposing my neck. The texture of its paw is rough against my cheek, but for some reason, its claws never graze my skin.

The animal lowers his muzzle, and I can feel hot breath getting closer and closer until finally, it takes a bite from my neck. I let out a high-pitched scream, but no one is around to hear me. I curl my hands into the ground, feeling my nails breaking against the concrete.

This is it; this is where I die. More tears run down my face with the realization that I will be taken from this world.

My skin feels hot and there's blood trailing down my neck. My face is wet, and my body feels like it's burning from the inside out. I can no longer scream; nothing comes out of my mouth when I try to speak. I'm like a fish out of water, my mouth gasping for the last bit of air to stay alive.

This is how my thirty-two-year-old ass will fucking die.

Feeling around the ground with weak and bloody fingers, I touch the smooth texture of the pocketknife. Finally, a bit of luck. It's cool against my burning skin. I grab it and stab the animal underneath its mouth. It yelps and gets off me, but before it fully does, I manage to get the big fucker in the eye. Blood streams down my face into my mouth. I spit it out and try to keep myself from vomiting. I get up quickly and take off, leaving the sharp blade lodged in its eyeball.

With one last look, I shriek, finally realizing that it was a wolf that attacked me. Grabbing my neck, I find blood. Not enough to kill me, but I'll definitely need a rabies shot.

While the animal is distracted with pain, I make a run for it, stumbling with shaky legs and not looking back again.

CHAPTER 5

Az

I'm sitting in the jeep with Tyler to avoid Benji talking for three fucking hours about who knows what. I love my brother, but I'm just so close to finding who I'm looking for that I can almost taste it, and it's putting me on edge.

So Ash gets to deal with Benji for now. They're driving in the truck ahead of us and we're following close behind.

From what Ash told me, we need to rescue this girl and her kids. We have no more information, only that her name is Katarina, and she has two kids, a girl, and a boy. They're going to be living with us for God knows how long.

I'm not thrilled about having strangers staying in our home. I don't trust new people easily because of all the shit I've been through. From what I've been told by the people that always try to diagnose me, my inability to trust is normal.

I'll just have to keep myself busy for a few days so I can purposely ignore the family.

Tyler watches me toying with my blade. If it were anyone else, they'd think that I was just a crazy person playing with knives, but not Tyler or the other two, they know me too well. "You okay brother?" he asks in concern, and I can almost see what he's seeing, the erratic edge to my movements that not everyone would pick up on. He probably thinks I'm about to stab someone and he wants to make sure it's not the girl.

I'm not sure why we're on an errand to grab a girl we don't know. The only reason I didn't fight harder is that it's in the general vicinity of where my investigation has taken me. That, and because when Amara's ancestors speak urgently, it means that we need to get on it ASAP, or else we are all fucked. But what's so important about this woman and her kids? They're not supernatural from the investigation Tyler did. They live in a cookie-cutter home in a suburban neighborhood; there's absolutely nothing special about them.

I laugh darkly. "Yeah, just in deep thought." If you look at us from the outside, you'd think that I could take my nerdy brother, but he's just as ruthless as me, Ash, and even Benji. Underneath his flirty ways, he's every bit of the killer that the rest of us are. I just wear my crazy twenty-four-seven, it has fewer people fucking with me. My brothers like putting on different personas to pretend to be somewhat normal.

"Yeah, I just want to get this shit over with so that I can finish hunting." I'm so close to finding the witch and I want blood. I press the tip of the blade a little too hard on my index finger and blood trails down my hand. I lick it off, finding the metallic taste calming.

As wolves, we don't find blood all that concerning the way humans might.

We finally get to the city and stumble across a lady staggering all over the place. "Probably a drunk," I say annoyed, not giving her a second glance.

Tyler stops the car and quickly pulls up the picture he

printed of the girl earlier today when he was doing his research.

"It's her." I sit up straighter and I really look at her now. Her shirt is drenched in blood, and she has one hand cupping her neck while the other clings to anything that can prop her up. She's stumbling through the street, and to any random onlooker, she looks like a druggie or a drunk.

Tyler shouts before getting out of the car. "Miss." He tries to walk over to her but she keeps running away from him.

I grab my phone from my pocket and look for Ash's number. "Where are you guys?" he asks as soon as he picks up. They were ahead of us on the road and didn't see when we stopped.

"We found her, but it's not looking good, man," I say, holding the sharp part of the knife tighter in my other hand, watching the blood spill out but feeling no pain. I'm more concerned about the scene in front of me.

"Talk to me," Ash says on the other side of the call.

I'm in disbelief when I say the next words out loud. "Someone turned her."

"What?" I can hear Benji in the background. He's just as surprised as we all are. This shouldn't have happened.

"Are you trying to tell me someone fucking bit her? Who would be stupid enough to risk our wrath?" That's the million-dollar question. "In our fucking territory." He's shouting belligerently.

"No fucking clue." Whoever did this is a fucking idiot that's for sure. The wolf inside me is begging to get out of the car and chase her down. I almost do, but we have to tread carefully, and everything I do is aggressive, so I'm not the best person to handle the situation. This is more of Tyler, Benji, or Ash's territory on a good day.

I can hear the screech of Ash's truck as Benji turns back

around. "Okay, we're doubling back to meet you." He hangs up and I put my phone back in my pocket.

"Miss. Please let me help you." This is the last thing Tyler is able to tell her before she runs off.

With my window rolled down, I lean my head out and watch as she leaves. She's actually pretty fast for a tuned wolf.

Tyler gets back in the car and a look of concern mirrors both of our faces.

"This is not good," Tyler says and I nod in agreement.

CHAPTER 6

KAT

I decide to run back home, although the diner is closer, my body isn't feeling so great, and I want to make sure that I'm not about to die.

Everything looks distorted. I walk and run, pausing when I can't handle all the shapes I'm seeing. I close my eyes tightly, hoping that it will clear away the haze, but it does nothing when I open them back up.

I stumble and fall through neighborhoods, using low tree branches and parked cars to help prop me up until I can focus enough to keep going. I probably look like I'm drunk.

"Miss," someone says. I want to cover my ears because of how loud the voice sounds. I look around but have no idea where it's coming from.

Is it my mind? Am I hearing things now? I shake my head to see if that helps.

Once my vision clears a bit, I start walking again. "Miss." There's that voice again, and I cover my ears feeling like it's going to make my eardrums bleed. "Please let me help you." I turn slightly and spot a man on the opposite side of the street standing in front of a car's bright headlights with a phone in his hand. I cover my face, trying to shield my eyes from the car's high beams.

Shit, he's probably calling someone already, but I don't want to stay here so I stumble faster. "Hey, wait up," he says, but I don't look back.

I'm still shivering from the cold, but now my body is burning up and it has nothing to do with how far I ran. I feel feverish and lightheaded, and as I approach my driveway, I can't focus. It feels as though the ground is trying to swallow me whole.

I hesitantly touch my burning neck, still surprised that I'm alive. I think I should be dead by the way I'm feeling. My whole shirt is wet with blood, but at least I'm alive.

A couple minutes later, I'm opening the door and going straight to my room, not stopping until I make it to the bathroom. I shut the door, looking at the bite in the mirror above the sink. I'm sweating profusely, probably because of all the running. Luckily for me, I exercise almost every day, so I was able to make it all the way back home.

"Mom, your home?" My ears are so sensitive. I grab my hair near the scalp trying to yank it off my head. "I thought you were going out," my daughter continues, not knowing how much her voice is affecting me. It sounds so loud even though she's standing on the other side of the bathroom door.

Shit, what do I tell her? I don't want her to worry. "I encountered a small problem and I had to come back home." It's vague, but hopefully it'll keep her from asking more questions.

"Can I go to Harper's house and study for our test? She can pick me up in five minutes."

I don't think about anything but getting her out of the house while I deal with everything. "Yeah, go ahead." Normally, I would ask her a lot of questions and then decide if it's safe to let her go. My overprotectiveness comes from knowing how evil people can be behind closed doors. I've encountered many of them living in foster homes, and I don't want anyone harming my kids.

Feeling light headed, I lay my back against the bathtub. "Okay. Thanks, Mom." Hearing her voice makes me want to peel my skin off. There's so much heat radiating from my body I can barely handle it. It's almost laughable that just an hour ago I was freezing.

"Take your brother with you," I manage to choke out. I need to be by myself for a little while longer trying to figure out what to do about the bite. I stand back up and go to the cabinet to grab some alcohol and cotton before it gets infected.

I pour the liquid onto the white ball and look at the nasty bite that's already turning purple. There are five teeth marks on the top and bottom almost forming an oval. I grip the counter tightly as I dab it once over the wound and nearly pass out in agony.

My neck feels like it's on fire. I shut my eyes tightly and try to keep myself from screaming by biting my lip so hard that it bleeds. The small trickle of blood runs down my chin and drips onto the counter.

"But, Mom—" she starts but I wave my hand and cut her off. I should probably call an ambulance to take me to the hospital. There is something seriously wrong with me. The fear of being taken away permanently from my kids is what stops me from calling for help.

"Either he goes with you, or you don't go at all," I manage to spit out, my voice hoarse. My throat feels raw like I've been screaming for hours.

"Fine," she grumbles.

I breathe a little easier knowing that they won't see me in this state of pain.

Maybe I should ask her for some water before she leaves. My mouth is parched.

I open my mouth to yell out but it's somehow impaired. As if I can't take any more pain, my bones feel like they're readjusting themselves. I watch my skin moving and my bones shifting inside my body. *How is this possible? I'm delusional.*

I'm crouched on the floor, but I don't remember how I got down here. Shock runs through me when I see my eyes glowing violet in the mirror on the back of the bathroom door. *What in the world is going on with me?*

I try to sit up but barely manage it. Still staring at the mirror, I notice my face reshaping itself. *What the fuck!* I try to talk again and sob when I can't speak. My mouth is transforming into a muzzle, and that's when I lose it and scream, but it doesn't sound anything like it should. My cry sounds more like a broken howl.

My bones crack and adjust into something different, and my fingernails are breaking apart. Everything in my body is crumbling, just like my life. My body convulses and I throw up the food that I had earlier with the kids.

My eyesight changes to something sharper, and frankly, it's scaring me. I'm not used to this. I no longer have normal legs and arms but stand on all fours. I can no longer see my smooth, sun-kissed skin, but a thick coat covers my body, so black it reminds me of midnight.

What the fuck just happened to me? Did I just get bitten and turn into a wolf? No, can't be, that's fake! Isn't it?

I look around the bathroom trying to figure out how to get out of here. I need to get some help. Jessica, if I can get to her, she might help me figure out what's going on. I just hope

I don't scare her to death. If the positions were reversed, I know I'd freak the fuck out.

With one of my hands—I mean paws because that's what they are now—I slide the window open and hop out, landing on the concrete with a surprising amount of grace.

It's pretty dark now so no one will be able to see me, but I'll stick to the shadows just in case. The last thing I need is to be taken away by animal control. Now that would suck. They'd probably take me back to the wild far away from my kids or put me down like a stray with rabies.

I try the first couple of steps to walk and end up falling to the side. I'm like a baby that's trying to learn how to use their legs for the first time. I get up again but the same thing happens and I huff in frustration. When I get up a third time, my walk flows better, and I pick up my pace until I'm running.

I run all the way to the diner in half the time it took the first time. When I get to the restaurant, Jess is sitting in our usual booth next to the window waiting for me with a cell phone in hand and a concerned look on her face. I wish I could tell her that I'm here, but the only thing I can do is howl for her attention.

I try again, but she still won't look at me. She glances around the restaurant, her eyes flitting from table to table hoping to find me sitting at one of them. She's touching her earlobe, something she does when she's nervous. She's probably thinking about the worst case scenarios in her mind. But she can't possibly guess what actually happened to me.

I need to figure out how to become human again. *Is that even a possibility? Can I be human again? I hope so.*

From the corner of my eye, I notice movement. Quickly turning my head, I find a group of four wolves hanging on the other side of the restaurant. They're staring at me with their teeth bared and a chorus of low growling meets my sensitive ears. They don't look friendly at all.

I may have only been a werewolf for five minutes, but I know that what they're doing is not a good sign. I slowly back away, keeping an eye on the aggressive pack of wolves.

"You better run."

I turn around to see where the voice is coming from but don't find anyone but those four.

I back away slowly, managing to get a good distance away from them. I turn my whole body around and sprint like a bat out of hell.

I pump my legs to keep going. Running this freely is exhilarating, but my body starts to slow down. Maybe with more practice I'd be able to run for a longer time.

It doesn't take long for them to catch up to me, taking advantage of my slower pace. Two of them are next to me. They're faster, but I keep running to try and outpace them.

Keeping my eyes straight ahead, I can feel them staring at me. I'm already exhausted. I take a closer look at the one on my left that is white as snow. If I weren't running away trying to save my life, I'd be appreciating his fur. He looks like this is a normal pace for him. I peer to my right at a beautiful red coat, and that wolf stares at me like he'd rather play than try to attack me. They both speed faster and end up in front of me, screeching to a halt. I debate jumping over them.

"We can't outrun them, they are just too fast for us. At least for now," the voice says again.

"Who is that?" I ask myself.

I'm surrounded by wolves, two in the front and two in the back. I come to a complete stop.

They get closer to me and begin to sniff as my body shrinks from fear.

"Don't show them any fear."

"Who are you?" I'm so confused right now.

"I'm your wolf. Who else would I be?" She scoffs in a sassy tone.

I'm speechless. Am I finally losing it? That has to be it. I've been put through the ringer today and I have finally reached insanity.

"You have a human side and a wolf side now." Umm... Okay... *"We can talk about this later. Right now we need to focus on destroying them."*

Wow. She's savage. My wolf side wants to fight them, but my human side is assessing our situation, and our odds and are not looking too great right now. The non animal part of me is terrified about getting killed and is going through scenarios on how best to approach this situation.

My wolf side seems fearless, believing that we can take them all down. I nearly take a step forward in a fighting position when one of them growls. I look back at the one that's snarling. It has a plush, golden-brown coat, and the one standing next to him has a darker brown coat.

The hairs on top of my body stand to attention when I look at them again. I start with the one with the red coat, then move to the brown, then to the golden-brown one, and finally, the white one. The intensity in his gaze has me wanting to put my head down and submit. It's overwhelming to say the least and it makes my wolf angry.

I don't realize when it happens until I'm flying in midair toward the biggest one, only to be dragged down. One of them catches my back leg before I make it far.

I'm whimpering on the floor with all three wolves on top of me and a pain so intense that it makes me want to claw out of my own body.

My wolf is so angry that we've been put down. I try to quiet that side of my mind and focus on the human side. It's no help though, that side of me is panicking so hard. I try to focus more on the animal side that tells me to bite and claw my way out.

I almost make it out of the three bodies until I hear a deep, rumbling voice. "Sleep." My body tenses until I realize what I'm doing, so I fight back again. No, this can't be happening. I can't be taken away.

Sleep. My body stills again. *Sleep.* And with that last word, my eyes finally close and everything goes black.

M y heavy eyelids finally lift open, waking from a deep sleep and feeling extremely rested. I can't remember the last time I felt this good. I look at my body and find that I'm human again. I bring my hands up to examine my fingers as if they're going to change into paws at any moment.

Did I dream that I actually turned into a wolf? Gosh, I hope it was only a dream. Maybe Theo leaving was a dream too. I almost started to breathe easier until—

"Nope, you're a wolf." There's that voice again. *"And that dick did cheat on you."*

I sit up for the first time and look at my surroundings. *Where the hell am I?*

I'm wrapped underneath a warm, cozy blanket, but when I realize I have no clothes on, I wrap myself tighter.

How did I get here?

Shit. My kids!

I stand right up on shaky legs but find I have no strength and plop right down on the bed.

"Careful there." My body tenses and my heart pounds

erratically. I cover myself up and immediately search out the owner of that playful voice. He's standing in the doorway. "Your body is tired. You should probably rest some more." I shut my eyes, cover my ears, and look down at the bed. He has a lyrical voice but it's so loud.

I lay my hands back on the mattress and look up again. I'm staring at a rock star. Well, I don't know that for sure, but he does look the part. He's a tall, lean guy, maybe six feet, with six-pack abs to die for. His pants ride low on his hips, and his t-shirt hangs from his back pocket. He has ink on his body but I try to remove my gaze from studying them. He has sleek red hair in an undercut style.

I might have stared at him too hard. "You like what you see?" he asks, leaning into the doorframe with his arms crossed and a huge grin. My face immediately heats. "You'll get used to it." I lift an eyebrow up. "The sounds, you'll get used to it." Oh, that's awkward. I thought he was implying something else. "I know your ears are sensitive right now."

So it did happen, it wasn't just a dream.

"I told you," the voice in my head says, and I can almost feel her jaw tighten. I'm starting to sense she really hates being ignored.

"Where…" My mouth is dry and I lick my lips before trying again. "Where am I?" He brings me a glass of water and I'm hesitant to take it. My hands seem to be working on their own because I nearly try to touch his body when he gets close to me. I pull my hands back immediately before he notices any strange behavior. I can't believe I almost rubbed that ripped body. It would have been inappropriate for me to do that.

"I promise this is just water." I get a whiff of pepper, amber wood, and citrus. This close, I can see brown freckles lining his nose.

His green eyes look sincere, and I struggle to figure out whether this is just an act. He places the glass in my hand and we briefly touch. The wolf part of me is now more alert, but I ignore whatever this is for now and tip the liquid down my throat, closing my eyes to suppress the urge to moan. The fluid runs down to my belly, and I swear I've never tasted anything sweeter.

When I open my eyes, the man is staring at me with a dreamy gaze, and I can't help but watch as his throat bobs up and down. He has his hands behind his back and his muscles look strained like he's avoiding trying to touch me too.

I finish the drink and hand it back to him. "And I promise we didn't touch you. To answer your question." That doesn't really answer my whole question, but I don't want to ask who "we" is because I'm not planning to stay. Or is that too harsh? Maybe I should thank them. But I have priorities.

"I need to get back home to my kids," I say, trying to stand up again but remembering that I don't have any clothes on and I have an audience. "Do you have any clothes that I can borrow?" Maybe "we" means a girlfriend, a wife, or a fiancé that has clothes I can wear.

"I don't have any at the moment, but Tyler is picking up your clothes." Maybe that's a girls name or maybe he's gay. Why do I feel a little disappointed at the thought that either of those might apply?

He watches me closely, and I try not to squirm against his intense stare, so I stare at him right back. After a moment, his smile widens. Well this exchange is…weird. I never thought having a staring contest would be amusing. I usually avoid people's stares when I can.

"My name is Benjamin but everyone calls me Benji for short. What's yours?"

That catches me off guard. I wasn't expecting him to give

up his name. So maybe he is being friendly and I'm the rude one.

"Katarina, but people call me Kat for short. How long will it be until Tyler comes back? I need to get to my kids. Do you have a phone I can borrow?" My voice still sounds a little raspy but the glass of water helps.

"I love the name Katarina." I really like the way he says my name. I shake my head to snap out of it. "But I'll call you Kat for short." He pulls his cellphone from his back pocket and hands it to me.

I immediately dial Ava's number, thanking the gods I made it a priority to always remember my kids' phone number and not rely on having my phone.

She answers on the second ring. "Hello." Her voice is unsure and hesitant since she doesn't recognize the number on the screen. I almost cry in relief as soon as I hear her voice.

"Ava, it's me, Mom." My hand shakes against the phone.

"Mom, where have you been?" she demands. I want to tell her everything, but I'm not even sure what happened. I think I'll wait until at least I know what's going on. I know that they'll have questions because I do too, but I don't know how to answer them yet.

"How's your brother?" I pray that he's there with her.

"He's here with me too, but why did you send a guy to come pick us up?" No, this can't be happening. Is it CPS? Did Theo call CPS on our children? No, he wouldn't do that, or would he?

Benji notices my reaction and quickly tries to calm me. "That's my brother. He went to pick them up." My shoulders fall, slightly relieved, but I have to know how they found out about who my kids are and why they would bring them here. Is it for my benefit or for theirs? "They should be here in an hour." My eyebrows scrunch up. How far away are we from the house? "We're about three hours away," he responds without me having to ask out loud.

"Is everything okay, Mom?" I'm not sure about that. I feel like Benji is being very vague and I'm being kept in the dark.

"Yeah, everything is going to be fine." I tell her with all the confidence I can muster. "See you soon. Call this number if you need anything." I look at Benji to confirm that Ava can call his phone and he nods his head, letting me know it's all good.

"Let me talk to your brother." I need to make sure both of my kids are fine.

There's a brief moment before his worried voice fills the line. "Hey, Mom. What happened? Why weren't you home last night?" I'm not sure how to answer that question.

"I think I passed out." I decide on a semi truth for now. I technically did pass out last night.

"I was scared something happened to you. We came home and you weren't there." I close my eyes trying to prevent tears from running down my face again.

"I'm sorry, Ezra," I say so softly, opening them back up and staring at the wall to avoid Benji's eyes. I don't want him to see my vulnerability. I barely know him, and something this raw is reserved for close people. "I can't wait to see you. I miss you and love you both."

"We love you too," he says before hanging up.

I look back at Benji and hand him his phone. "Thank you."

"Anything for you." And I can't help but blush again. This guy is a real flirt. I bet he has women begging for his attention. I've got to keep my eye on him to make sure I don't fall for any of his tricks. "In case you were wondering, we didn't tell your kids about you being a wolf." I sigh in relief.

I'm glad they didn't say anything. I should be the one that tells them what happened.

"The shower is right in there," he continues, pointing to another door that's connected to this bedroom.

A shower sounds great right about now. "Uh, thanks."

"Your clothes should be here when you get out of the shower." I'm so grateful someone is getting me clothes. The only setback I have is not having money to pay them back for all of this. As soon as I find a job, the first thing I'm doing besides finding an apartment and buying a car is paying them back.

Benji laughs but I have no idea what is so funny. "You know, my brother doesn't normally run errands, but he personally felt the need to go pick up your kids." I tilt my head to the side puzzled, but he doesn't clarify further.

I throw my legs off the side of the bed and tighten the blanket around my body cautiously. "I'm going to go shower now," I say, hoping that he will get the hint that I'd like privacy. Yet he still stands by the door unfazed.

"Okay." He sounds excited.

"And I'm naked," I say

"Yes you are." He crosses his arms and lifts the corner of his mouth in a smirk.

"I kind of need you to leave so I can shower." I cross my arms over the blankets mimicking him.

"One day you'll invite me in, Kat." Doubtful. He walks away, but not before giving me a sexy wink. Yeah, I have to watch out for that one. He closes the door, and when I don't hear anyone else, I walk into the bathroom to get cleaned up.

I'm impressed by the size of the tub. It would be a shame to not use it to its full potential, so I decide to take a bath instead. I start the water on the hottest setting and flinch at the noise. I hope I get used to the loud sounds soon.

I turn to the mirror on top of the sink and look at my body, noticing a tattoo of a wolf on my side that wasn't there before. I wonder if all wolves have something similar.

I have faint scratches on my skin and the bite still looks red, but not as bad as yesterday. I touch it and gasp at the burn, *motherfucker.*

My human side shivers at the thought of turning into a wolf. I need to ask how this wolf thing works. I look through the cabinets and find a couple of bath bombs. They smell like lavender and a hint of almond. I grab one and throw it in, watching as it fizzles.

When the water fills up and the sweet aroma fills the bathroom, I sit down and relax. It's hot enough that my skin feels like it's going to fall off.

I try not to think about how much my life has changed in twenty-four hours, but it's hard not to.

I'm a wolf now, I can't believe I'm actually thinking those words.

I wonder if it's contagious. Can I give it to my kids? How many wolves are out there? There are so many questions I need answered.

I also need to figure out the job situation. We have four days now to vacate the house with all our belongings and no place to live. I feel like a failure. I have no clue what I'm going to do now.

"Wolf, are you there?"

"Of course I'm here. Where else would I go? I'm a part of you." I can almost feel her rolling her eyes at me. Strangely, I'm starting to feel at ease with my wolf, almost like she's been with me my whole life.

I remember what happened to us last night and decide to bring it up. "So…you wanted to attack the white wolf and now we end up here." I cross my arms waiting for an explanation.

My wolf huffs, and I feel as though she crosses her arms too, or maybe that's why I crossed mine. Ugh I can't tell anymore.

"Well, we could have taken one of them out if you had resisted the command of one of the Alpha's." I scoff, she's acting like this is all my fault.

"I doubt we could have taken one out, let alone four." I grab a bottle of shampoo that's off to the side. It smells like honey and cinnamon. I wash my hair and dip my head in the water.

"We could have taken them," she says with so much seriousness.

"You're going to get us killed thinking that way. We've got to assess the situation before we attack." I grab the conditioner and put more than I need on my long, dark hair.

"No, you're going to get us killed if you don't trust me."

Instead of sounding annoyed like I thought she would, she's whining, clearly enjoying the massage as much as I do.

I wonder if everyone talks to their wolf like this or if it's strange behavior.

"Ask the wannabe rockstar."

"I think the 'rockstar' style fits him quite nicely." She ignores me, continuing to enjoy the bath.

As I rinse my hair, there's a knock on the door. It startles me from my thoughts and the inner dialogue I'm having with myself. "Your clothes are here," Benji says, and I relax again. "It's on the bed when you're ready." I hear him walk back out and close the door softly, and I know he did that for my benefit.

I quickly wash my body while the water drains and get

out of the tub. There's a towel hanging just outside of the bath, so I dry myself and wrap it around my body.

When I open the bathroom door, my eyes widen and my mouth hangs open.

There are bags upon bags of clothing sitting on top of the bed, and I know that the clothes are expensive because it's what I usually buy. Surely this is not for me because if it is, this is going to be hard to pay off. Maybe I can take the least expensive clothes and ask them to return the others.

I grab some boy shorts, a bra, a pair of pants, and a shirt and put them on. So I'm wearing about seven hundred and fifty dollars worth of clothes right now. Normally that wouldn't mean anything to me, but since I've gotten kicked out of my own home, I feel uncomfortable wearing what I can no longer afford.

There are some nice flats and I decide to wear them too. There's another knock on the door. Benji sure is quiet when he doesn't want me to know he's approaching. "Are you dressed?"

"Yeah, you can come in." I hear the doorknob twisting. It's going to take some time to get used to the amplified sounds that I never paid attention to before.

"You look great," he says with a huge smile. "But if I'm being honest, I thought you'd wear something different." I know what he means. I'd usually pick the most expensive outfit that would look great on me, but since I'm low on funds, or to be accurate, have no funds, I have to pick the most affordable out of the batch. I cringe when I think about how much I have to pay them back.

My wolf reacts to his compliment and wants me to give him a shy smile.

"Didn't you say he was a wannabe rockstar?" I scold her. *"I've changed my mind."*

I ignore her for the moment and look down at the clothes. "Umm…yeah I'm going for the comfy look. Besides, I don't think I need all of this," I say, pointing to the pile of pretty bags sitting on top of the bed.

"Oh." My blood turns cold, and I know that whatever he's going to say next, I'm not going to like. "Kitty Kat, you're moving in with us," he says it like it's a fact.

I jerk my head back. "What?" Maybe I am being kidnapped! Fuck! And I just brought my kids right to the wolves' den.

Chapter 8

Kat

"Can you repeat that again, I must have misheard you?" Yeah, that's probably it. My sensitive hearing probably just didn't catch on to what he said. There's no way he said what I thought he did.

He scratches the back of his head. Clearly nervous about my reaction. "You're staying here." I cross my arms and look up at him, even though I'm way shorter than he is. The energy I'm giving off is as if I'm looking down at him. "It's probably best if Tyler or someone other than me explains it. Except for Az though," he chuckles, "that one would be absolutely terrible at explaining this. But the other two are better at this shit than I am." He grabs his phone from his back pocket and looks at the time. "Ash should be here any minute now."

Before I can rip him apart, I hear two sets of footsteps running down the hall, and boy are they loud, or it could be my sensitive hearing.

My kids walk in the room. This room is big enough for ten people to fit here comfortably. I'm wondering if I'm in the master bedroom. I look around at the open space. It sure feels like it.

I hug them both, grabbing one in each arm. "I missed you both so much."

"So who exactly is Ash, and why did he say we needed to pack our belongings? Ash said we were going to stay here permanently. Is Dad coming to stay with us?" I let go of them and clear my throat, wondering how I'm going to explain all of this to them.

"I'll be outside." Benji makes a run for it. He probably wants to avoid the huge bomb he just dropped on me. "Yell if you need anything, and I do mean anything," he says with a small, sultry smile as he leaves the room. My wolf perks up at what he was insinuating.

"Calm down girl," I tell her. *"We're probably being kidnapped."*

"Are you dating that guy?" Ava asks, crossing her arms and trying to look intimidating just like me, but of course it doesn't work because I'm her mom. Maybe it works on other people but definitely not me.

"To answer your first question." Here it goes. The kids are going to be so heartbroken. He might not have cared for them, but that's their dad. I'm sure they'll miss him. "Your dad and I are getting a divorce." I look down at my shaky hands. "He gave me five days, well now four, to find a job and a place to live."

"Dad is with his assistant, isn't he?" Ezra says more like a fact than a question. "She was always hanging around Dad way too close." He stares off into space like he's putting together the pieces. Then he looks at me again.

"Unfortunately, yes. I am so sorry for you two." I tell them sadly. I feel like this is all my fault. Maybe I should have tried harder to keep my husband happy.

"Mom, stop apologizing. This isn't your fault. I secretly think he's never liked any of us. I think he just wanted to put up a front and show that we were a family since you know…" She stops like I know what she means. When I don't say anything, she throws her arms in the air in frustration and continues. "A family lawyer, that's the only reason he tolerated all of us. He never took us out anywhere and never cared about anything that we did. It was always you, Mom."

Was I so deeply in love with Theo that I never saw the signs? Was he not a good father like I always thought he was?

I thought he couldn't make those recitals or the school open house or any other events we had because he was hard at work providing for his family. Was this all a lie that I made up in my head to justify the way he treated us?

"Yeah, he never cared about anything we did. Every time I'd try to talk to him, he'd send me away." With every scenario they'd bring up, my guilt grows stronger and stronger. I was supposed to be their mother and take care of them and watch over them. Have I failed my kids? I don't think my broken heart can take more of their stories, but I listen anyway because it's something they need to get off their chest.

When they're finally exhausted Ava says, "Mom, I'm going to miss my friends." I know that my girl is popular at school. Boys are always eager to talk to me and try to convince me to let my daughter go on dates with them. I have always turned them down because well, I was a teenage mom, and I don't want that to happen to my daughter. It was a hard life, but once Theo opened his practice, life was great, or so I thought.

"I have no idea what we're going to do," I tell them both sincerely. "I'll try and see if we can find a place close to your school or at least ask for a transfer. That way you two will not have to switch schools." It's the least I can do since the transition might be hard for them.

"Ash is pretty sure that we're going to stay here with him. He said that we will love it here. The school is amazing and the people are nice," Ezra says almost like he admires the guy. I'm going to have some words with Ash when I find him. How dare he make choices for my family. He doesn't know us at all.

"Yeah, Ash is pretty freaking awesome. I can't wait for you to meet him and he's also…" She looks around to make sure no one else is in here and whispers, "he's pretty hot too." She winks and laughs. "All I'm saying is, I wouldn't be mad if you moved on and dated him or the rockstar." I'm taken aback by what my daughter says, and she cackles at my horrified look. "He does look like he would be in a band. Ash also said there are kids our age here too. I'm kind of excited for a new change."

I have to put a stop to this before it goes any further. I put my hand up to keep my kids from talking. "Okay, hold up guys. Nothing has been decided yet, and I need to find a job first." Where is this damn Ash guy? I really need to meet him and give him a piece of my mind. Who does he think he is ordering my family around like that?

"But Mom, have you seen this house? It's huge. It's like five times bigger than our old house. I can't wait to get in that pool," she says, jumping up and down with glee.

Before I talk again, another man comes into the room and I'm drooling.

He's the very definition of tall, dark, and handsome. He has dark brown skin, and when he smiles, there's dimples on both sides of his cheeks making him look irresistible.

My wolf stirs. I can't seem to take my eyes off him. His dark brown eyes are full of mischief. He's the same height as

Benji and I want to see what is underneath the pants and shirt he's wearing. If the way his clothing fits him is any indication of his build, I'm going to like what I see.

"Mom!" Eva shouts, breaking the spell I was momentarily under.

I look back at my daughter, "Huh?" I ask with my brows dipped low in confusion.

"He asked you a question like five minutes ago and all you've been doing is ogling his body." She gives me an exasperated look.

I should be embarrassed, but I can't help it. I'm walking forward without realizing what I'm doing. It's like he's using an invisible thread to pull me toward him. I can't help but gaze at that beautiful smile of his.

"Hey, I'm Tyler." His voice is deep, dreamy, and alluring. Instead of extending my hand, I trip over a bag that has fallen over on the floor and see the ground where my face is going to end up.

Tyler is quick and manages to grab me and pull me up, but instead of pulling away, I lean into a hug. My wolf wants to be close to him and stay like this forever.

I catch a whiff of an expensive cologne, cinnamon, cedar, amber, and a hint of vanilla. I can tell because I've bought many for Theo over the years. He also smells like the outdoors, precisely a forest and rain, the same smell as Benji.

He holds me up in his strong arms, running his nose across my neck. I can't help but tilt to the side giving him better access.

"Okay, this is weird," my son says, and I'm startled enough to immediately pull back from the hug.

I clear my throat trying to compose myself, but I know my cheeks are reddening to a scarlet shade. "Hi, sorry about that. My name is Katarina, but people call me Kat."

"Well I'm not," he chuckles seductively, which shows off his sexy dimples and his perfect white teeth. He's clearly talking about the hug, right? This is so strange. I don't know what to say, but the urge to go back and smell him is so strong, just like it was with Benji. I put my needy hands behind my back to prevent me from trying to touch him further and embarrassing myself even more.

He clearly notices the tight grip I have on my hands and chuckles. "Hey Tyler, I'm Ava and this is my brother, Ezra." Oh right, I forgot to introduce my kids. "My mom is clearly drooling all over you so she forgot her manners," my daughter says sweetly, avoiding me and the daggers I'm clearly throwing her way.

"Don't worry, I'm used to ladies staring and throwing themselves at me." He shrugs and my kids laugh at his joke, but he's clearly playing…I think.

"Let me show you all to your rooms," he says as my kids follow.

"No wait," I say before he leaves. "Thank you for everything but we're not staying."

He gives me another huge smile. "I don't think that's an option for you." With that, he walks away with my kids, leaving me alone in the room once again.

CHAPTER 9

BENJI

I just met the most beautiful girl in the world. Her dark brown eyes are so alluring. Her black hair is so smooth that I want to run my fingers through her silky strands. Although she's perfect, she's really skinny. I'm sure she'll put on some hips once she gets a hold of Lily's cooking.

I have to control my wolf when we're around her. He's pacing back and forth like a caged animal trying to be let out so that he can smell her. He loves to be near her. We both do.

I know that there is no mating connection because it was taken, not only from me, but from my brothers as well. But I feel like this is close to it. If I didn't know any better, I'd think this would be it.

But once she hears about our fate, she may no longer want to be with us.

I hear the kids walking to see their room and I head outside to meet Ash.

"How are the kids? They seem excited for a new change." I watch him inhale his cigarette. He only smokes occasionally and usually when he's really stressed out. I think we're all a little on edge. Especially because the council will hear about this soon, and when they come after her, they'll come after us for keeping secrets.

The council is not something you mess with. They rule over all shifters, and although we have our own territory, we still have to abide by the laws of those ruthless leaders.

I really hope the dumbass who turned Kat can protect her. If not, I know that I can't leave it up to fate. I wonder if Kat knows the consequences of being turned and she chose to ignore them.

"The kids are fine. I showed them the pool and they were sold. Theo was a piece of shit father. I have a strong feeling they're going to like this place, even if they're not supernatural. My gut is telling me they'll accept people for who they are and not for what they are." He puts the cigarette back to his lips while inhaling. "How is Katarina doing?"

I think about how surprised she looked when I told her she was staying. "I don't know, Ash. I don't think she knew about being a wolf. I think this might all be new to her." Ash lifts an eyebrow, not convinced that she didn't have a hand in all of this.

"I think she had a boyfriend on the side and he just made her a target. If we find the boyfriend we should kill him," Ash growls as he exhales. I agree with him, but it has nothing to do with the council and everything to do with how much I want Kat for all of us.

"I think a change of scenery and lifestyle will make her realize that he wasn't good for her." I'm answering for both the boyfriend and the husband. "But I accidentally let it slip that she was staying with us."

"How did she take it?" Ash lets out a cloud of smoke.

"Not great at all." When I think about the fear in her eyes, I wish I could have comforted her and not left her so confused. "Did Amara say how long she's staying here?" I ask, watching Tyler jogging from the forest to meet us, probably checking on the camera's surrounding our property.

"Not sure. Maybe indefinitely now that we know she was bitten. It's not safe for her." Ash disposes his old cigarette into the ashtray, reaching into his pocket and grabbing a new one. He twirls it around his fingers the exact same way Az does with a knife.

"Since you're going to talk to her soon, can you tell Amara to put a strong spell surrounding the property and a spell to keep her here?" Ash reaches into his pockets pulling out a lighter and lighting up his cig.

"Yeah, I'll go ask her." I say without thinking it through.

"If you're going to put up a spell to keep her here, we should probably let her know. We don't want her scared if she tries to leave and finds out she can't," Tyler says, walking closer to us.

Ash rubs his chin thoughtfully. "No she's already scared, we'll let her know later."

"I'll go tell Amara," Tyler says. "You should probably get Kat so she can talk to Ash. She's freaking out about staying." My wolf gets excited about seeing her again.

Ash pulls a phone I don't recognize from his back pocket and lifts it up. "I forgot to give this to the kids, but it's been ringing nonstop. It's driving me insane. Can you give this to Katarina before I throw it against the wall just to make it silent?" he mumbles while he hands it to me, but Tyler is quicker and snatches it.

"I'll give it to her right now." I wonder if his wolf wants to see her as much as mine does.

"I thought you were going to go talk to Amara," I say, giving him a pointed stare.

"I am, but I'll give Kat her phone first." He stares at the

name on the screen. "Who is Dan?" My wolf and Tyler's growl at the same time.

"No fucking idea, just get rid of that phone for me," Ash says, putting out the cigarette.

Tyler rushes inside the house to give Kat her phone, and I'm a little jealous at not being the one to give it to her.

"Benji, be careful. We don't know enough information on her." I know that he's my brother and wants to look out for me, but in my heart, I feel she's something special. Maybe not quite like a mate but close enough.

"I don't think she's dangerous, Ash, I think she's different," Ash grunts in response, obviously not believing me.

We head back inside. Ash goes into the office and I go check on my Kitty Kat.

W hat does he mean that's not an option? This is really starting to feel like they're holding me and my kids hostage. They seem friendly, but you never know what lies underneath those beautiful faces. Maybe it's a facade to hide who they truly are. My body slightly shakes at the thought.

"And how is that possible?"

"Well, I don't know, maybe…magic. If being a wolf is possible, why wouldn't magic be a possibility? Maybe these supernaturals talk to one another." I hear a wheezing sound and look around to see where it's coming from when I realize that it's me. I'm doing this weird laugh. Well, my wolf side is, and I think she's cackling at me…us…argh. I can't keep it straight anymore.

"Mom?" I look at Ava's concerned gaze. "Are you okay?"

"Huh?" I scratch my head trying to come back to reality. When did she come in? "Yeah, I'm fine sweetie." I try to give her a reassuring smile but she still looks skeptical.

"Okay…" she drags out, looking at me like I've lost my marbles. Maybe I have. I'm a grown-ass woman who got cheated on and dumped only to be bitten, made into a wolf, and brought to this house by two sexy men, only for them to tell me that I can't leave this place.

Any woman in my position would go crazy. I think I'm handling this situation better than most adults would.

"What is it, Ava?" I ask, remembering she came in here for a reason.

"Oh, nothing." She backs away toward the door like I really am a lunatic, but she has a goofy grin which lets me know that she isn't actually afraid of me. Thank goodness. I just hope that they won't be scared when they find out what I am now.

When I can no longer hear her loud-ass feet, and I'm sure there are no more prying eyes, I go back to thinking more about my situation and the ungodly amount of questions I have running through my brain.

I wonder how their hierarchy works.

And who is Ash?

Is he the one these guys answer to? Are they mad because I nearly attacked one of them? I didn't mean to; my wolf got the best of me. She was angry, and truthfully, so was I, but she's quicker to react than my human side. I haven't figured out if that's a good thing or a bad thing yet.

"We could have taken them," she argues, but it's less fierce than she was before. I think she has a thing for the guys.

I just realized I haven't seen the house yet. I decide to venture off and see where the hell I am and maybe find an escape for my kids and me if they are really holding us hostage.

I walk out of the room for the first time and into a huge hallway with rooms on both sides. I don't hear Tyler or my kids, so they might not be close by.

I debate whether or not to open the room closest to me, but curiosity gets the best of me, and I turn the knob expecting it to be locked. With my defenses up, I swing the door open, but instead of a threat on the other side, I find a messy room just as big as mine. The only thing that's clean is the bed with a guitar sitting on top of it.

From the smell alone, I can guess this room belongs to Benji. His guitars line the back wall.

I don't know what possessed me to take a shirt from the floor, but I take the band tee that's laying next to my feet and hold it up. The Doors. He's got good taste in music, and it still smells like pepper, amber wood, and citrus, so exactly like Benji. I hide it underneath my shirt. *Maybe he won't notice,* I tell myself.

"Yeah, sure, that's inconspicuous," my wolf says. I look down to see what she's complaining about. I find the band tee poking through the side of my fitted shirt and it makes me look like I'm pregnant. It definitely looks like I'm hiding something. But…maybe he won't notice. I mean by the looks of it, he's got a lot of shirts all over his room. I don't think he'll miss this one.

I close the door, still curious about all the other rooms. The next one is cleaner and smells just like Tyler. He has large computer screens all over the room that would make any nerd jealous. He has a comfy chair in the center of the monitors. He must be some type of tech whiz.

There are pictures of what I assume are his family on the desk. He stands in between his parents smiling at the camera. His dad has the same sexy dimples as Tyler, and his mom has an easy smile. He gets his good looks from both of them.

I look around the room, definitely not planning to steal anything until something catches my eye. A hoodie that says *Mystic Shadow Academy*, and it smells just like Tyler. I'm sure he won't miss this raggedy old thing, so I take it with me and hide it on the backside of my shirt.

"Oh great, now it looks like you're pregnant in the front and the back. Still think no one will notice?" She rolls her eyes at me. *"Why don't you just ask them if they'd give you something that smells like them. I'm sure they'd willingly give us something."*

"Umm...because that would just be plain weird," I retort.

"Oh, so taking their stuff without them knowing isn't strange?" She smirks.

"No," I say simply, knowing damn well this is stealing.

I walk out and go to the next door down the hall, which is next to mine, and open it. I faintly recognize the smell of jasmine, nutmeg, ginger, and lavender from one of the wolves last night. This room is in complete order. Not one single thing is out of place. Even Tyler had a few things on the floor. It's like whoever stays in this room is a neat freak. There are no family pictures, so I can't really get a sense of who this guy is. He has a pair of hand-cuffs sitting on the side table next to his bed. I think this person might be into kink, and my wolf yelps with excitement.

"Down girl," I tell her. *"Remember, we aren't planning on staying."*

I quickly walk to the closet only to find that it's closed and locked. I sit on the bed trying to figure out how to pry it open, but as soon as I feel the soft surface, all I want to do is lie down on the bed and roll around in it. There's an added touch of lavender. I really like this one's scent. Is that weird? Do wolves act this way?

I get up to walk back out and explore some more, but as soon as I hit the hallway, I miss the smell already. I quickly go back into the room and grab a pillow from the bed, closing the bedroom door as I'm leaving again.

"This might be harder to hide."

"You think?" she snorts.

Back in my room, I pull my finds from my shirt and toss them on the bed. I put the pillow to my face, taking in the scent again. This is weird, right? I gently place it back down on the mattress and hide my treasures behind it. At least the stolen pillow doesn't look out of place, but I have to make sure to hide the other two items. Knowing I have one more room to explore, I go back down the quiet hallway to the last door.

I twist the knob to enter but find that it's locked. I try it once more, hoping to pry it open, but it won't budge. I use all my strength, which is a lot stronger than what it used to be before I turned into a wolf, but it doesn't move. What are these doors made of? Curiosity burns through my body, but I know I have to check on my kids. There is nothing else here for me to explore, so I walk across the hallway instead, passing a long, grandeur staircase. I try not to squeal like a little girl, but this place is so exciting. I've never been in a mansion before.

I keep walking past bedrooms until I hear my kids' voices. Their rooms are across from each other, and they're shouting back and forth loudly.

"Hey, Mom!" Ava exclaims, jumping up and down. "Come look at my room." I walk in after her. "I have my own bathroom," she says excitedly. "I don't have to share with dirty-ass Ezra anymore."

"Hey!" I hear my son shout. "I heard that."

"Watch your language, Ava." Her room is smaller than mine but definitely bigger than what she's used to. I look out of her window and am surprised to find a balcony, but it's not nearly high enough off the ground to keep a determined teenager in her room. We can't stay here, and even if I wanted to, I can't afford this place.

I look around her room and am surprised to find five suitcases worth of stuff. Ava notices the look on my face as I stare at her luggage. "Ash told us we weren't coming back so I needed to pack everything I couldn't leave behind." She looks at her luggage longingly like she wishes she could have fit more stuff in those suitcases. "He told Ezra and me that they would buy us what we needed to decorate our room." Absolutely not, but I don't tell her that. Instead, I give her a tight smile, which she takes as a good sign.

I turn around and face the hallway. My son waves me over excitedly and I walk to his room. "My room is going to look so awesome when I'm done with it," he says, looking around his spacious bedroom. It's the same size as Ava's. I look at the luggage on the floor and he has the same amount as his sister.

There's a knock on the door and I turn around to see Tyler leaning on the doorframe, his presence taking over the space in the room. My body immediately reacts as I move closer.

He has my phone in his hand. "Ash gave me this before he left. He said it's been ringing nonstop." I snap out of it and grab my phone. There are dozens of missed calls from Jess on the screen when I unlock it. "Shit," I say out loud, then cover my mouth before swiping my phone again. She's messaged me over a hundred times frantically asking if I'm okay. Oh no, no, no she must be panicking.

There are a few from Dan. He's Theo's best friend and a sweetheart. He's probably worried about me. I don't want to talk to him about what's been going on, especially since Theo and I broke up. They're best friends and he doesn't have any allegiance to me.

Eventually, I'll call him, but not today.

I run back to my room, noticing how easy it feels to run now, and I close the door immediately to dial her number. She picks up on the first ring. "Kat, where the hell are you? I've been freaking out nonstop. I went to your house and no one was home."

I'm not sure how to tell her what happened to me. I don't want to lie to my best friend. I'm not sure where to start, but this is a conversation I don't want to have over the phone.

"Sorry, I didn't mean to scare you." I grip the phone tighter than I mean to, then loosen my hold because I don't know if being a wolf comes with the extra strength powers all the books talk about.

"Where are you?" She brings up a good question, which I'm still trying to figure out.

"I'm safe." At least for now, maybe I should have waited to call her. Now she's going to worry about me since I'm being so vague. Maybe this is worse.

"Why do I feel like you're hiding something from me?" I sigh because I am. I just don't know how to tell her because I don't know what's going on myself.

"Just tell her the truth," my wolf grumbles. *"The truth will come out anyway. Might as well save your time and energy wondering how she's going to react. Either she'll accept you or think you're crazy."*

I ignore that side of me. "I'm fine now. Let me call you later." I say, hoping that will keep her from asking more questions.

"Okay…" She sounds hesitant. "This conversation isn't over, but I'll let it go for now. If you don't want to talk about it right now that's fine, but just know I won't let this go until I see for myself that you're doing fine." I knew it wouldn't be that easy with her. I expect no less from my best friend. "Call me if you need anything."

"I will," I say quickly. "Bye, Jess."

"Bye, Kat." I hang up the phone feeling guilty that I didn't tell her about my wolf, but how do I explain this when I don't really understand what's going on?"

"See, you should have just told her the truth. Would have saved us both the stress and headache of wondering how she'd react."

"Hush," I tell my wolf.

"You know I'm right." I can feel her glare.

"Hush," I tell her again.

I sit on my bed and stare at the floor as if it has all the answers I'm searching for. My life has changed so much in just twenty-four hours. Just yesterday, I saw my husband having sex in our bed with his assistant. Then I get bitten and turn into a wolf, and now I'm told I'm going to live here by some guy I haven't met yet. I'm still betting this is payback for trying to attack one of the wolves. But, what else do they expect? It was four against one.

There's a huge shadow outside my door, and I look up to see Benji staring at me. My breath picks up. He has his signature smirk, or one that I can associate with it being only his. He has one leg crossed over the other in a relaxed pose.

When I acknowledge him, he walks in and sits next to me. I still can't believe how he moves so silently. That's why I can never pick up when he, or even Tyler, are walking.

He reaches over and grabs my hand that's laying on my lap and draws soothing circles over my skin. My body relaxes. I wasn't aware I was so tense. "I know it's a lot, Kat, but things will get easier. I'm so happy you're staying with us now." Yeah, I'm not too sure about that. He tucks my hair behind my ear and my head automatically leans into his hand. What the fuck am I doing right now? Why am I leaning into him?

I'm surprised my wolf is quiet and not giving her opinion on what she thinks about him, but I think I already know she wants to get closer, despite wanting to start a fight with them yesterday.

It's an effort, but I pull away from Benji when I hear heavy footsteps in the house. Being able to hear like this is definitely going to take some getting used to, and I wonder if that was done for my benefit. "That's Ash, he told me to take you downstairs to his office. He wants to talk to you." Finally, I get to meet the guy who decided that I'm staying here without asking for my permission.

We get up and walk through the hallway down the stairs. There are so many rooms throughout the house that I know I'll be getting lost in here. I suck at navigating, even when I have Google Maps on, I always manage to miss my damn exit.

I follow Benji and can't help but stare at his tight butt. "You like what you see?" My eyes shoot up straight to his, and I'm not going to lie, I'm a little embarrassed for checking him out. I mean come on; I'm still married. Even if Theo doesn't want me, I still feel like I should respect him since he's my husband, even if he doesn't do the same for me. It doesn't make any sense, but it's just the way I'm wired.

"Idiot." My wolf sounds annoyed, and I know she's right.

"Uh…sorry." I try to look anywhere else but his face because I just outed myself. I should have lied and came up with something to save me from this awkwardness.

"I'm not," he says, extending his hand to turn the knob. He opens the door and…oh shit. My wolf perks up, even if she does try to hide it. These men have a strange effect on us.

"Kat, meet another Alpha of the Iron Beast Pack, Ash." My jaw drops to the floor.

CHAPTER 11

KAT

y mouth hangs open and my heart rate picks up.
I know that I just scolded myself for checking
out Benji, but I can't help it with these guys.
Does this place only house good-looking people? Or good-looking wolves I should say. Or are they shifters? Does it even matter?

God, I can't think straight.

The man standing on the opposite of the desk is an absolute god. He has platinum hair that's cut in a sleek, mid-length style that frames his beautiful face.

He's the same height as Benji and Tyler. He's not as brawny as Tyler but has a stronger build then Benji. My body automatically moves toward the desk. My hand reaches out to touch him, but I catch it before it becomes weird—if it hasn't already. My hand is already out so I extend it further, pretending it was meant as a handshake. What is it with me and trying to throw myself at these guys? I hope it doesn't happen with every guy I meet now. If that is the case, I'm going to have a really hard time getting to know people.

I finally look into his eyes, and the power he radiates is so strong. "See if they know anything and report back to me, Az." He hangs up the phone.

His eyes are a soft blue with hints of green; they remind me of the beaches of Oahu.

My body wants to kneel before him. I don't even breathe for fear of having to bow down instead. I keep my body locked into place, making sure I don't do anything stupid. I've never encountered so many awkward situations until today.

With my hand still outstretched like an idiot, I smile and say, "I'm Katarina, Kat for short, and no we are not staying." I add a little friendly smile at the end to soften the blow. He's wearing a scowl, but even that makes him look sexy. What the fuck Kat, keep it together? Just because you're getting divorced soon, doesn't mean you have to look at every guy you meet like a piece of meat.

His mouth twitches in annoyance and looks down at my hand like it's going to bite him. I try not to flinch from being turned down, knowing that all I want to do is rub my hands all over his body.

"*Yes we do,*" my wolf chimes in. I'm so glad no one can hear our banter or she would have outed me by now.

"My name is Ash," he says with an air of authority. Benji and Tyler, although Alpha's from what I can tell, don't act so arrogant. "And yes, you are staying here, Katarina." He emphasizes my full name like I didn't just tell him to call me Kat. The dominance he's radiating is starting to make me lightheaded. The power coming out of him is so strong I'm starting to think he's doing it on purpose to intimidate me. I'm not sure if that's right, but it sure feels like it.

Well, he doesn't know who I am. I don't go down without a fight. Well, unless you're Theo, apparently. He pulled my heart out and stomped it on the floor like it didn't mean anything to him. My eyes start to well up and I blink quickly, pushing those thoughts away and trying to focus on what's in front of me. Because with this guy standing across from me, you need all your energy and focus.

I finally put my arm down since he has no intentions of touching me. "I don't know who you think you are, but no, I'm not staying." I say it in my most terrifying "mom" voice hoping it will work for this arrogant asshole. I mean, does he really think he can just keep deciding for my kids and me when I've barely just met him? "If this is about me attacking you last night, I am sorry about that. I'm new to this world and my wolf took over."

"You didn't come close to touching me." Umm...okay. This guy is so full of himself.

"Is this a challenge?" My wolf hums excitedly.

"Calm down," I snap back. We would probably be killed if we even tried. Although my wolf loves a challenge, I like to keep it safe. I prefer my body in one piece and not shredded by sharp teeth and claws.

My wolf scoffs. It's as if he can tell what just went on with me and my wolf, his eyes swirl and change color. I think mine do the same because my vision changes, as if I'm now looking through a different lens.

He stumbles back for a moment, but I don't pay it any further attention because my wolf whines, and I bite my tongue hard to keep my mouth from opening. *"Chill girl,"* I tell her. *"Remember, we hate him, and we tried killing them."*

"Mine," is all she says.

"Fuck that," I snap.

"Step aside, I'm taking over." I don't need her accidentally mating with this guy. I'm not sure if that's even possible, but it's what I've read in all my fantasy books. Although, if he didn't want to shake my hand, I doubt he'd want to "mate"

with us. She grudgingly moves aside and my human side takes over.

He continues talking, not even noticing I had an internal debate with myself. "Yes you are, and this is not up for debate." The nerve of this guy. Who does he think he is?

"Well, I've got to go," Benji says out of the blue. I almost forgot he was still here. I must be really pissed because it's hard to forget Benji's presence.

"You should probably stay," I say without looking at him. "You might have to hold me back if I try killing Ash here." I stare daggers into the man in question as he gazes back at me with the same murdering energy.

"Our living arrangements just got livelier," he says with a chuckle. I hear a door open and close, leaving the two of us alone in this room.

We don't dare move our eyes from one another, even if my body still wants to bow down to him. As I pay attention to my wolf, something must have crossed my features. I see a shadow of his wolf and the look of excitement in his eyes. Oh shit, I have no idea what that means, but when they go back to his normal, bored look, I'm not sure if I imagined it.

"Don't give in. Keep challenging him," she says, and for once, we are both in agreement.

I get an idea. "If this is punishment for last night. I'm truly sorry." I try a humble approach. "I promise to stay out of your way." I bat my lashes and give him the sweetest smile I can muster. This works all the time when I'm trying to get out of a speeding ticket or when I want someone to do something for me. It's even worked on Theo a few times. This should be no different.

"No." I open my mouth to talk but he cuts me off. "So how are you going to navigate being a werewolf? Do you know how to change willingly and how to change back? How to control yourself during the full moon? How to not accidentally turn someone into a werewolf?" That hasn't crossed my mind yet. My kids, I can't let this happen to them. When I don't answer, he continues smugly, knowing he's got me there. "You need a pack, and if I don't claim you, another pack will."

"I'm sorry what?" He makes sense about accidentally turning my kids, but the rest is gibberish. I'm just not sure I want to admit to the cocky guy in front of me that he might have a point about the kids' safety. I know that I can't navigate this wolf myself.

"No one has been turned in the last century." His eye twitches slightly, almost as if he didn't mean for that comment to come out. I want to ask more questions, but he continues. "We usually stay in packs. We're a family. There are some that roam as lone wolves, but they can get picked on by other packs and get killed." Well, that doesn't sound reassuring.

"Okay, so I stay here until…" I say, dragging it out.

"Forever." He shrugs as if that's normal. I'm currently panicking inside. I don't know if I want another commitment, especially if it's a lifetime one when I'm currently working on getting out of the one I have. "Plus, we are the best pack around. Why wouldn't you want to stay with us?" he says smugly. "Or is your boyfriend going to come get you?" What boyfriend? I've only ever had one boyfriend and that was Theo.

I draw my brows together. "I don't have one. Do you mean my husband?" But he doesn't look convinced.

"Is your husband a wolf?" I shake my head. "So who turned you?"

"Oh…I actually don't know." I shrug.

"Then why did you get turned?" He crosses his arms like he's trying to catch me in a lie and it's irritating.

"I'm wondering the same thing." I mimic his movements.

"I find that hard to believe." I roll my eyes at his rude tone.

"First off, I have no clue who bit me or why. I really don't know why someone would want to turn me into a wolf. I thought it wanted to kill me, not turn me. Maybe it missed and turned me instead of killing me."

"Then you're up for grabs." What the hell? He says it like I'm an object or something.

"Again, I get to decide that." My life is not up for debate.

"Fine, by all means, go ahead and walk out the door. If you don't claim us as your Alpha's, someone else will, and they'll be more forceful. It's rare to survive that bite, so this makes you special. You'll always be a target."

It's rare to survive that bite. My body shivers, knowing that I could have died. He's got me there, and if that wicked smile is any indication, he knows it.

I take a long moment before answering because this is a lifetime commitment. Do I even have a choice? I have no idea how to be a wolf or what comes with the territory. I wish I wasn't so in the dark about all this.

I sigh. "Can you teach me more about being a wolf?" Then remember another thing that's just as important. "Can you help me find a job?" If he wants me to stay so badly, then I can have him help me look for work.

He touches his heart. "As one of your Alpha's, I will make sure you know more about your new species, and yes, I'll help you find a job." I can't tell if he's mocking me or being sincere. I look at those blue-green eyes, getting lost in the beautiful color until he speaks again. I find myself having to snap out of it more times than I'd like. "You and the kids can stay with us."

"Who is us?"

"You've met Benji and Tyler. There is one more Alpha that lives here, Aziel...uh Az." He recovers quickly and I don't think he meant for that to come out. "And you and I have met already."

"So just the four of you in this big house?" I ask looking around the room. His office is huge with books stacked behind him. The desk and chair look expensive, as do the portraits hanging on the wall. These guys must be loaded.

"Well, not anymore. It's you, Ava, and Ezra too." He walks from behind the desk and casually leans over the front of it. I'm itching to get closer to him but stand completely still not wanting him to see how much he is affecting me. He's already too cocky. I don't want him knowing how much my body responds to him.

Living here is going to be the death of me. All I want to do is run my hands over all these guys. "There is one thing left to do," he says, getting up and standing right in front of me." I look up at him and swallow hard. His closeness is making my mind foggy.

"And that is?" I whisper when he leans his face close to mine. My wolf is alert, wanting me to reach up and touch his beautiful face.

"We need to seal the bond so that we can become your Alphas." My heart thumps loudly and I know he can hear it. My cheeks redden from the thought of him knowing how much it's getting to me.

"How do we seal it?" I ask huskily.

He grins like he knows what his closeness is doing to me. "With a kiss." He brushes the rim of my mouth so softly with his that it leaves me hungry for more. "Are you ready?"

"Mhmm…" I can't form a coherent thought when he crushes his lips to mine. My whole body reacts to him. He lifts me up and sets me on his desk, not pulling away an inch. I fist his soft strands of white hair while opening my legs wide for him.

I don't know what takes over my body, but I want more than this. Is it bad to think he's a better kisser than Theo? Or that I feel more from this kiss than I ever had before?

He settles in between my legs using one of his hands to rub against my thigh. I can smell the sweetness of his arousal and I'm certain he can smell mine. I'm glad the feeling is mutual. I would have been embarrassed if I were the only one that felt this way.

There is a bond that forms right from my heart to his, and I hope I don't come to regret this.

His phone dings and he pulls back too soon, but I can feel the strength of the connection we just formed.

He takes a step back and I try to make sure no clothing is out of place.

"So, is this how everyone joins your pack?" I ask, my voice breathy while I straighten my clothes.

"No, we normally do a blood oath," he says casually, and I stop what I'm doing to look up at him, knowing that I look utterly dumbfounded.

"Then why the hell did we just kiss?" I point to his lips and then to mine, showing him exactly what I'm talking about as if he doesn't already know.

He shrugs before answering. "I wanted to see what you taste like."

"What for?" I narrow my eyes accusingly.

"Research purposes." I want to ask him what that means, but there's a knock on the door that startles me away from Ash while he's looking down at his phone.

The door opens. "Food is ready," an older lady says. I stand there awkwardly when she comes up to me with a wide grin. "You must be Kat," she says enthusiastically. She comes to hug me like we're old friends. She's about five-foot-six and around her sixties. I can smell the outdoors on her too, so I know she's a wolf.

I hug her back. "Yeah I'm Kat. It's nice to meet you…" I trail off so she can answer with her name.

"Lily. I'm the cook for the guys." We pull away. Yep, they're loaded. I thought we lived a pretty good life. We ate at fancy restaurants but never had a person that cooked for us. I always did all the cooking when we didn't go out.

"If not for Lily, we would forget to eat." Ash looks at her with a kind smile like she's more of a motherly figure.

"Good thing you guys have me then." She winks. "Your kids are already devouring the food I made. You two better get there before they eat everything." She looks at Ash. "You know your brothers will eat your plate too if you don't come now." Brothers?

Ash's hand hovers on my lower back as we walk out of his office following Lily. He's not actually touching me, but I can tell exactly where it is when he pulls away and leans close to my ear, his hot breath tickling my neck. "You taste like sweet cherries." I look at him as he sticks out his pink tongue and licks his lips slowly. I immediately turn away, not wanting my body to betray me again and for him to smell my arousal. Especially because I'm sure Lily sensed it while we were in his office. He's too cocky already, and I bet he has lots of women begging for his attention. He doesn't need another one, let alone an almost divorced one.

"So are they your brothers?" I ask when we walk into the dinning room. They look nothing alike. Ava, Ezra, Benji, and Tyler are already devouring their food.

"We don't have the same parents if that's what you mean. But they're my brothers in more ways than just blood. We have stuck to each other since we were kids. We've been best friends since we were young." I'd love to hear that story. "We're just missing one, but he should be in tomorrow night." He sits at the head of the table while I sit next to him. I'm facing Benji and he gives me a sexy smile before he dives back into his food. Tyler sits next to him. Ava sits to my right, and Ezra sits next to her.

"Mom, this is so good," my son says with a mouthful of food like he can't get enough.

"Yeah, so good," Ava agrees. Well that's a first, they're always so picky.

I'm excited to eat when I look at the plate in front of me and gasp loudly. Everyone stops what they're doing to stare at me.

"Is something wrong?" Ash asks, annoyed that I've interrupted their meal.

Yes.

I've never seen that many carbs in one plate. It's going to take me a long time to burn all those calories. Speaking of, I didn't get to exercise yesterday or today. Theo wanted to stay under thirty carbs, so my plate always consisted of healthy foods. I also exercised nearly every day because he wanted me to be fit. Although that didn't help with my hips, once I had my babies, my body just wasn't the same. I think he secretly hoped that my body would return to the way it looked when he first met me.

"No. Everything is fine." I pick up my fork and stab the mashed potatoes. Everyone goes back to eating except for Ash. He looks at me intently, probably worried that I'm going to stab him in the back with my knife when he least expects it. He might be right.

I hesitantly shove the potatoes into my mouth, they are buttery and oh so flavorful.

I mentally count the carbs I'm consuming out of habit. If I only eat some of my food, I might only have to work out about an hour and a half. I wonder if they have a gym somewhere here. Or I could just go out for a run. This place is a mansion, they should have a nice neighborhood to run in, right?

Everyone gets up from the table and leaves. "I'll be in my room unpacking," my daughter says.

"Me too, but I'll be playing video games," Ezra says with a cheeky grin. I nod and give them the go ahead. They get up, taking their plates to the kitchen with them as they go.

It's just Benji and me and he's still staring with a frown. I get the urge to fill the air with chatter. "Food is delicious. Lily is such a great cook. Where is she anyway?" I never saw her come back to the table.

"She's probably out getting more ingredients for dinner. She's cooking for three other people now." He moves to sit next to me, resting his elbows on the table and his head underneath his hand. I have no idea what he's thinking, but it can't be anything good by the face he's making.

"Oh, great." Maybe she won't see me throw the rest of the food in the trash. I don't want her to feel bad. Her cooking is great, it's just I can't remember the last time I ate a hearty meal like this.

I get up from the chair, and as I reach for my plate, Benji holds on to it, preventing me from taking it. Maybe he's being a gentleman and wants to take the plate himself. Him and Tyler seem to be kinder than Ash. "Where do you think you're going?" Or maybe not? Did I have this all wrong? Do I have to watch my back with him too?

"Well, I was going to take my plate to the kitchen to clean

it," I say, trying to pick it up again, but he has a tight grip on the edge.

"You barely ate." He draws his eyes with concern. "It's lunch time and you skipped breakfast."

"I ate enough." I look back at my almost untouched food.

"If you don't eat, I'm going to make you sit on my lap and spoon feed it to you." I stare at his face to see if he's being playful, but he looks serious.

"No you're not, and I'm done." With his other hand he moves his plate and puts mine in front of him. In one swift movement, he sits me down on his lap. "I guess we'll do this the hard way," he whispers in my ear.

I'm too shocked to react. Under all our clothes, I can feel his muscular, fit legs as one strong, tattooed arm encircles my waist.

My mind is mush when I'm this close to him. He's like a drug that I want more of but refuse to give in to because of Theo. Living with him and the other two is going to be hard. Let's hope the other guy isn't this attractive.

He grabs a spoonful of macaroni, which is the only part of the meal that I didn't touch, and brings it to my mouth. My eyes widen but I keep my lips tightly shut. "Challenge accept-ed," he says in that playful voice of his.

I can't think of the food when I feel his length underneath me. Maybe I do want something to eat, but it's not what I'm being fed. Fuck. All I want to do is rub my ass against it.

"When did you get your tattoo?" he asks, bringing me out of my cloudy mind.

"Oh, um." I touch the heart tattoo just underneath my eye. "My best friend and I got it before I got married. It was some-thing for me to remember who I am and where we came from." Which I guess I forgot after I married Theo since I basically let him control every aspect of my life.

"Did you forget?" His eyes are sincere but curious.

"Yes," I say sadly. Distancing myself from my husband, I can see that he had me wrapped around his finger.

This close to Benji, I almost want to reach out and touch the side of his face but keep a tight grip on my hands. My wolf is no help; she keeps wanting me to do it.

"So, about my nice, round butt," he starts. I open my mouth to say something when he shoves the food in quickly. I was so distracted I didn't notice when he grabbed the fork again. I narrow my eyes but savor the rich and creamy cheese sauce. It's been a long time since I've had this.

He feeds me a couple more bites and I don't care that this looks weird at all. When I can take no more food in my belly, he pushes the plate away.

"Is there a gym here?" I ask hopefully.

"Yeah, we have one." Yes! I try to get off his lap so he can show me where, but he holds on to me tightly.

"If you're worried about gaining weight, we have a high metabolism and often go running in our wolf forms." Oh, well that's good to know. "Can I ask you why you're divorcing your husband?" That catches me by surprise.

"He…" I stutter. "He was banging his assistant in our house." I look down at my shaky hands feeling ashamed. "In our room. He gave me less than a week to find a place and a job."

He lifts my chin up and I look into his eyes. "You've got a place here now. You don't have to worry about not having somewhere to live. You and the kids are part of the pack." I hold back my tears. Maybe this is a good thing, a blessing in disguise. Having a place to stay solves half my problems.

"Of course, it's a good thing you've got me now," my wolf says and I chuckle internally.

"Let me show you around this place. It can be a little daunting." I bet it is. "We've got three hundred acres and the south side of the property borders the state forest that's connected to the Wenatchee National Forest." My mouth hangs open. This place is bigger than I thought. "I want to show you where you're going to be working." I sit up straighter with the word work. When did Ash and Benji talk? That was fast. When I demanded Ash find me a job, I didn't think he'd actually talk to his brother about it. But I can't say that I'm not grateful.

"Yeah…that would be great." I'm so happy at the idea of being able to finally make money. Theo provided me with everything and told me that I didn't need to go back to school after he built his practice, and now I'm left with no skills and feeling like a failure.

Whatever this job is, even if it's cleaning toilets, I'm going to do it with such pride. It's been a long time since I've made my own money, and I'm excited about being able to provide for my kids and myself.

"I'm ready." He finally lets me get up from his lap, taking my plate along with his to the kitchen. I trail after him, and the smell of sugary sweets hits my nose.

"I'm making you guys a pumpkin pie for dinner tonight." Lily smiles as she continues to stir together ingredients. I can almost taste the sugary dessert in my mouth. I'm definitely grabbing a piece later. The grocery store is probably not too far if she already made it back.

The kitchen is just as big as everything in this house, with more cabinets and drawers than I've ever seen. I'm amazed at how huge this place can be, especially because I always thought of our home—Theo's home—as a big place.

Thinking of Theo brings a sharp pain to my chest, and I can't help but wonder what he's doing right now. Is he happy? Does he regret what he did now that he's living in the aftermath? I pull my phone from my back pocket to check if I have any missed calls or messages, but there's absolutely nothing from him. I try not to let that bug me, but it tugs at my heart.

"Are you ready?" Benji asks. I put the phone back in my pocket before I start bawling my eyes out again. I'll do that in private, away from any prying eyes.

"Yeah, let's go." We walk outside and I get my first real look around the area. I stand in front of the house admiring the white walls and Spanish architecture. "How many rooms does this place have?"

"Sixteen." Damn, we only had four and I thought we lived like rich people. "We have a pool too. The kids were so excited when they saw it. There's also a tennis court and basketball court."

There's a jeep parked right in front of the house with Tyler in the driver's seat and my kids in the back. They roll down their windows and wave. "Hey, Mom," they shout in unison.

"We're going shopping," Ava says.

Before I can say anything, Benji intercedes. "Don't worry, it's on us." He winks and then grabs my hand. There's a tingle that shoots all the way up my arm. His hands are warm in mine, and I can't help but notice how perfectly my hands fit in his. "Come on, we're driving the truck. They're probably getting big furniture."

I follow him to the garage. There are about eleven cars here. "Who owns all of these?" I'm currently eyeing a classic, cherry red car. Letting go of his hand, I walk up to it, careful not to get too close. It's so clean and shiny.

"That's a 1956 Ford Fairlane convertible and it belongs to Az." I'm practically drooling over it. I want to take that beauty out for a drive. "And to answer your first question, these cars all belong to us." I need to figure out what these guys do for a living because I want it.

"What if they're hitmen? Would you do it?" I don't answer for a long moment considering the possibilities. *"You're actually thinking about it?"* My wolf shouts at me with amusement.

"Well, we need the money. I'd take anything," I tell her. She chuckles darkly. *"Nah, I don't think I'd be a good one anyway. I don't have the patience to wait around."*

"You forget you're a wolf now. We're hunters, and we've got nothing but time and patience when we're hunting our prey." My body shivers because I know she's right.

I pull my gaze back to Benji, watching him walk up to a lifted Chevy Silverado and open the passenger side door. As I'm reaching for the door handle to hoist myself into the cab, he grabs my waist effortlessly and sits me down on the seat.

My wolf side approves of his kind gesture. She likes that this male is taking charge, but I'm starting to think she might be some kind of ho since she likes all the other men in the house too.

"Our pack lives on this land. You could say we have a small community on our property with all the families that live here. We also have businesses inside this area." I look around and spot houses here and they're all as big as Theo's, but none of them are as big as Ash, Tyler, and Benji's place.

Our drive is silent while my mind races with thoughts of last night in the alley. Eyeing Benji's throat, my hand darts to my own subconsciously. "Were you bitten too?"

He looks at me and smiles. I gaze deeply into his emerald green eyes, letting them pull me right in. He glances back at the road, driving with one hand on top of the wheel. "I was born like this and so were my parents and my grandparents before them. We come from a long generation of wolf shifters." If I didn't see myself turning into a wolf, the idea of shifters existing would have me running for the hills. I think he notices my surprise because he continues. "We have existed since the beginning of time." My eyes widen and he laughs at the shocked expression on my face. "So, this is the very first time you've heard about supernaturals, huh? Did your boyfriend not tell you he was a wolf?"

"No, I don't have a boyfriend." I tell him slightly irritated for bringing it up again. Ash must have told him something about this. "I don't even know who that guy or girl was or what he wanted with me. I haven't had a boyfriend since Theo, and he is…was my husband," I correct myself. "We haven't filed for divorce yet, but because he's a lawyer, he's probably already working on drafting everything he needs to get me to sign on Friday."

With his free hand, he rubs his chin thoughtfully, causing

my heart to beat fast—and not in a good way. "What?" I practically shout. I don't like the look of concern on his face.

"So can I take you out on Friday?" My body goes completely still. He tries to play it cool with a grin on his face, but he's shifting slightly in his chair with unease. I can see that it took courage for him to ask me out, but I'm surprised. I wasn't expecting that question. "I mean, after you sign those papers, you'll be a free woman." The way his voice shakes is barely noticeable, but I'm paying too much attention. I can tell he isn't used to getting no for an answer, but he's afraid I'm going to turn him down.

What catches me more by surprise is my response. "Yeah, I'll go out with you Benji." I have no idea where this bravery came from, but I like this girl. Maybe everything will be alright after all. This new me is fearless.

He lets his head fall back in relief. "We're going to have so much fun, Kitty Kat," he promises, and my heart skips a beat. Finally, something good to look forward to on Friday.

I've been thinking about Ash's comment earlier and being able to control when I shift. I don't want there to be any accidents. "How do I make sure not to accidentally turn someone into a wolf?" I ask, carefully looking at his reaction.

"Well, technically you can't turn anyone unless you're an Alpha and there's a full moon." I'm about to break a tooth by how hard I keep grinding. I'm going to murder Ash. "But turning someone is dangerous. You usually need a couple of wolves to help with the transition, but you did it all on your own." My body trembles thinking about what happened yesterday. "How you survived by yourself is a mystery." He grabs my hand in his and heat creeps over my cheeks. "But I'm so happy you did. I only wish we would have found you earlier." It would have been nice to have someone on my side, but I don't know if I would have felt uncomfortable changing in front of people that I didn't know.

"There are some...rules," he hesitates. "One of them is to not turn any humans, and that's been in place for a while."

"Why?" I ask, curiosity taking over.

He takes his hand back and rubs his face. "The council rules over all shifters." Oh hell, that doesn't sound good.

"I thought you guys ruled here?" I lift my brow.

"We do. This is our territory, but there's also a council that we all need to listen to."

"Are there more rules to follow?"

"Plenty, but it's the hunters that will get you when you least expect it."

My throat goes dry and my eyes widen in shock. "I'm kidding, calm down," he chuckles. "Hunters don't exist anymore."

I narrow my eyes on him, annoyed at how casually he can joke about life-threatening situations. Before I can demand answers about the hunters, he changes the subject. "So, there is one female to every four males." I drag my eyes away from him and stare at the window so he doesn't see the sheer panic in my eyes.

So, am I expected to have kids? I always wanted more children, but after Theo decided on his own to get a vasectomy, I'd given up the possibility. Still, I can already feel the pressure building in my chest. How the hell can any woman keep four men satisfied? I couldn't even keep one happy.

As if he knows where my mind wanders off, he continues. "You're not expected to have kids or to even have a mate, and by our standard, you are really young." He knew exactly what I was thinking, that having kids at my age is pushing it.

I scratch my head and look at him again. "What do you mean by young?"

He chuckles. "I'm over two hundred. Lily is over three hundred."

My mouth hangs open and I compose myself quickly. "What the fu…"

"We're here," he announces loudly before I can finish my sentence.

Chapter 13

Kat

This conversation isn't over, but I'm intrigued by the shops that surround us. This place reminds me of a town in Leavenworth, Washington but twice as big. The town is a German town and it's pretty popular during the holidays. There are a lot of cute shops and dining places.

This little community has its own charm. I unbuckle my seatbelt, and before I can open the door, Benji is already there opening it for me.

Again, my wolf is pleased at how attentive he is. I think it's written all over my face because I see his eyes change with a hint of pride crossing his features and his chest pumps up. I try not to think too much about what the hell is going on.

I slide from the truck seat into his waiting arms, and he sets me on my feet just as his phone rings. His face falls. "Sorry, I have to take this." He climbs back into the truck and presses the phone to his ear. I almost want to ask if everything is okay but know that it isn't my business. If he wants to tell me, he will.

I hang outside looking at all the dessert shops and restaurants that I'd love to try. The sweet smell of donuts and the spicy aroma of Mexican food assaults my senses. I can't wait to come back and try these places as soon as I can afford them.

It doesn't take Benji long to finish his call, and he grins wide as he comes to stand next to me. I'm drooling over him when I hear someone in heels practically run toward us. "Hey Benji." I glance up to see a gorgeous woman with short black hair and hazel eyes batting her fake lashes at him. I've loved every single voice that I've heard so far, which is weird to admit. With sensitive ears, I can hear so much more than I used to. It's been the guys' voices mostly, except for Lily's, but this woman's voice makes my ears want to bleed.

She leaps up to him and gives him a lingering hug. As she clings to him, her short dress rides up and nearly shows the bottom of her ass cheeks. I feel like a bum standing next to her and really regret choosing such a plain outfit this morning.

When I open my mouth to speak, I'm surprised to hear a growl come out instead. The woman pulls away, giving me a nasty glare.

I cover my mouth with my hands in shock.

"What the fuck was that, wolf? Couldn't you have been more discreet?"

There is amusement dancing in Benji's eyes. I put my hands back down and he grabs my right one, putting it close to his chest. My wolf gets excited about this display, but my human side doesn't know what this means and feels absolutely embarrassed.

"Kat, meet Brooke. She's a member of our pack." I'm usually nice and friendly, but with her, I keep my lips shut, not feeling particularly kind. My wolf is on the edge, and I can feel my body wanting to shift just to attack her. I'm starting to shake violently, and claws emerge from my fingertips.

Benji nuzzles my neck and breathes into my skin. I have no idea when he hugged me from behind, but my whole body starts to calm down. Staring into her eyes, I know I'm giving the same vibe Ash was giving me earlier today when he wanted me to look down, but I refused. She glares daggers in my direction, and I see her wolf get angry watching me. Her eyes glow like she'd like to kill me for taking something that's hers. The feeling is mutual, bitch.

The tension in the air is high as a big body moves to block my vision. I look up to see Tyler's dimples staring down at me. "Hey Kat," he says, lifting his arm and touching my face tenderly. There's a shadow of his wolf and it looks like he wants to come out and play, but mine is still on edge, although it helps having their bodies close to mine.

After that realization, I snap out of it. What the hell just happened?

I step away from Benji but end up sandwiched between both guys. "So…" I was going to say sorry, but I don't want to apologize to Brooke. Instead I say, "I need some fresh air." The guys back away and there's hurt crossing Tyler's features. I want to hug him and nuzzle his neck the way Benji did for me, but this is just too weird. I can't think clearly. I need to get away.

I look through the stores lined up on the street and spot a boutique. I make a run for it because, if I know anything about my daughter, I know that she likes to shop. She's probably tried on dozens of outfits by now.

After passing many clothing racks, I go straight to the fitting rooms, finding Ezra in a chair looking bored out of his mind playing on his cell phone.

He looks up from his phone. "Oh hey, Mom. Ava convinced Tyler to take her here first." I bet she did.

"Ava, honey, I can't afford to buy you any new clothes. I haven't gotten a job yet." I look at one of the prices on the rack and flinch. Even when I do have a job, I probably won't be able to afford this.

"Tyler said to put it on their account and they'll take care of it." There's no hiding the pure excitement in her voice. She's always loved shopping just like me, I suppose.

"Yeah, that's not happening. They've already given us a place to stay, and we all have our own rooms. I don't want to be any more of a bother."

"It's no bother at all," Tyler says from right behind me. These guys are deadly silent. Maybe they really are assassins. He takes a small step but keeps his distance, though I kind of hope that he'll get closer.

"Look, you guys have been generous, but I just can't let you buy us these expensive clothes." All I can think about is how I'm going to repay them for all of this. It's bringing up old anxieties from my childhood when my foster parents didn't buy me anything and I had to figure out how to pay for clothes, school supplies, and anything else I needed. I never once thought I'd be in this situation again.

"Why not Mom?" Ava whines. "They bought you stuff." I wince because I know I need the clothes. Every time I think about going back and getting my things from the house, I feel nauseous. I don't want anything more from Theo.

"I'll tell you what," Tyler starts. "How about she works for it?" I pinch the tip of my nose, processing what he just said.

That's not a bad idea. "What do you have in mind?"

"She could work here." That might actually be a great

idea. I just hope she doesn't come home with new outfits every day.

"Yes, I'd love to work here," Ava says from the other side of the dressing room door.

He looks around the store until he spots someone. "Hey Ruby, can you come here for a moment?"

A tall woman in a flowy, rose-printed dress approaches us with a friendly smile. She looks to be about my age, but after Benji told me about their ages, I wonder how old she really is. "Yes Alpha?" She bows her head respectfully, and I can't help but wonder why she doesn't just call him by his name.

"You don't have to call me that in our pack. You can just call me Tyler."

"Thank you," she says with her head still bowed in submission.

"There's a sign that says help is needed." Tyler talks softly to her, and I wonder why he's being extra careful. "Can Ava apply?" She comes out with a handful of clothes and a giddy smile, and I already know she's taking the mountain of outfits home with her.

"Yes…" she stutters. "I need help Tuesdays and Thursdays."

"I would love to work here," my daughter chirps.

"Can you start next week after school?" It's Tuesday today, so she'll have time to settle in before she starts school. Speaking of which, I have to talk to Ash about school.

Ava looks at me for permission and I nod my head and smile. "Yes I can," she says excitedly.

Ruby looks relieved. "Great. After school for four hours." My daughter nods her head. She's been asking me if she could get a job for a while. "If you're ready, I can check you out."

Ava walks with a bounce in her step. I look at my other kid and he's still engrossed on his phone.

"There you are, Kitty Kat." I turn to look at Benji's smirk. "I'll hang out with the kids. I promised them shopping after all."

"No, I—"

"Ash is waiting for you outside, he's going to show you around and where you are going to work," he cuts me off.

"But my kids are my responsibility."

"Mom, we'll call if we need anything," Ezra says. They probably just want a little freedom to be by themselves without their mom hanging over them. It's hard to think they don't need me as much as I need them.

"Okay well, I'll have my phone with me if you need anything." I reluctantly walk away slowly, almost hoping that one of my kids will call me to come back, but they don't. I don't know whether to be scared or proud that they want to be on their own.

Chapter 14

Kat

I meet Ash outside and find Brooke standing next to him. I pinch my lips together, pinning her with a hateful stare. Something about that woman raises my hackles, and if the look she's giving me is any indication, she obviously despises me as well.

She runs her fingernails up and down Ash's skin and I try to calm myself. Taking in a deep breath, but all it does is irritate me more when I smell her scent mixing with his. I thought by now she would have left. If this were high school, I know I would have already beaten her ass for even looking at me the wrong way. As an adult with kids, I'm trying to act civilized, even if I am close to snapping. And despite the evil smirk she gives me, I can smell the fear on her.

What is happening right now? I choose to ignore her, anger simmering on the surface.

"I was told you were going to show me to my new job." My voice is snippy, but I don't care right now. My wolf is trying to bare her teeth. I look through my reflection in one of the store's windows and my eyes are glowing violet. What the hell? Am I not a normal wolf? Why is it different from the guys?

Normally this would be freaky for me to notice my eye color change like this, but fear is far from what I'm feeling right now. Right now, my mood is more murderous. This should shock me, but surprisingly, it doesn't. I want the taste of blood, but not just anyone's. I want hers.

My wolf believes Brooke is taking someone that belongs to us, and I'm working overtime to try and tame her.

"I've got to show Kat her new job," Ash says gently as he grabs her arms that are practically stuck to him and puts them down. He gives me none of that gentleness as he stares into my eyes. I can't tell if it's lust or disgust, and at this point, I don't even care.

"Don't forget you're coming to dinner tonight." She emphasizes those words to get a reaction from me, but I swallow my retort bitterly, refusing to give her the satisfaction of getting under my skin.

Ash's body tenses like he wasn't expecting her to say that. "It'll just be me tonight, the guys have to run other errands." She pouts her lips and reaches to give him a quick kiss on the lips. He looks startled, but I walk away, not caring if it's in the wrong direction. If I don't put some space between us, I'm going to beat both of their asses.

"Mine," my wolf growls.

"No," I say. *"Not mine. They don't belong to us."* I don't know what's wrong with me or why I feel this violent. It has to be my wolf side, but even so, I have no claim to this man or any of them for that matter.

"How did you know it was this direction?" He looks at me a little too intently like he believes that I'm still hiding something from him. Like I'm actually a spy and have been learning their territory, which is ridiculous, but looking at Ash, I can tell that he thinks it's a possibility.

"I didn't, I just started walking," I growl.

"Let's go this way. He points to the opposite side of the street. I want you to become familiar with this place." His tone is laced with a slight hint of venom, nothing as sweet as he was when he was talking to Brooke. This man doesn't like me at all.

"Fine," I say, crossing my arms over my chest while we walk in the direction he wants to take me.

"Don't get too cocky. Benji flirts with anything that has boobs and an ass, and Tyler is too kind to be rude to any woman." Wow, can this guy be any more of an asshole? "You're nothing special, Katarina." I tighten my fingernails on my arms, creating tiny crescent shapes on my skin. I stand corrected, this guy can really make a woman feel special.

Once I've calmed down enough, a smug smile creeps back over my face. "Well, why would Benji ask me out on Friday?" I question. He wears a scowl and it's his turn to tighten those fists. He says nothing else, and I feel like I've won this challenge.

We walk in silence the rest of the way. I have no intention of making small talk with him, and I try not to think about how insecure I am about the whole date on Friday. Now I'm wondering if it's his personality just like Dan, Theo's best friend, and maybe he was only trying to be kind to me. But no, he looked really nervous when he asked me out. It has to mean something, right?

After we cross a street, we make it to a big building that looks like a bar. He stops walking and opens the door for me. Surprisingly, my wolf feels more irritated than giddy at his gesture.

"This is where you're going to be working." I stare at the

neon purple sign, Crescent Lounge, written in cursive with a crescent moon in the background. It's all really elegant, and if I saw this place on the street, I'd think this lounge would be somewhere rich people go.

Once we're through the doors, I look around in surprise. This place looks nice, kind of what I would expect a club to look like. There's a bar with a shit ton of alcohol on one side, and the tables are filled with people eating. "It's a bar and restaurant, and the dance floor is over there." He points to an area on the opposite side of where we stand. "The second floor is the VIP area and a lounge." I look to where he's pointing. Yup, this place is definitely for rich people and celebrities. I love it.

When I turned fifteen, Jess got us fake IDs and we used to go out partying every night at dance clubs before Theo and I became an item. It was so much fun. I loved dancing. We were drinking and dancing with random guys for six months straight before meeting Theo. It was the most fun I ever had.

Dancing was a way for me to get loose and leave my torturous life behind for a while. It was a way to escape alongside the music.

Once I got married, he never wanted to go out dancing. I longed for those days though. Maybe I'll come here and dance if they play music on my off days.

We walk away from the dance area to the wall with all the liquor. "You'll be working in the bar."

"Oh, umm…" I fumble through my words. "I actually don't know much about alcohol." Besides those six months when Jess and I were going out, I've never really drank before. Occasionally I drank the wine offered at Theo's work parties, but that was just a sip here and there to be polite.

"I've got this cheat sheet that should help you navigate through drinks. You'll also have someone else with you, so you won't be alone, and if you have to, there's always google." He hands me the sheet and I look through the different drinks. "Usually, our customers order from this menu though. Benji will be here helping you out. But tonight you'll be waitressing." I whip my head up so fast in his direction. I wasn't aware I was starting tonight, but I guess today would be as good as any. I need to start making that money after all.

We walk to the far back corner of the bar. "We have an office here and upstairs." He opens it and it's not very big. It has a desk with some papers on top and drawers lining the back wall.

We go upstairs and...damn, have I mentioned how nice this place is? It's dark and seductive. "Over here is the lounge for people that don't pay for the VIP." It has tables surrounding the area and chairs set up. We walk to the other side. "This is the VIP lounge. People usually pay big money to hang out here." I didn't think the VIP area could get nicer, but I stand corrected. The place is lined with plush purple and black seating and pillows. I want to sit in one of them to see if they're as comfortable as they look, but I'm afraid if I do, I'll never want to get up. The walls are decorative with hints of purple. The tables overlook the dance floor and bar. This section has its own personal stairs that lead straight to the drinking area.

I walk further back and find two rooms that are closed off to everyone, even the VIP guests. There's a table in the middle with purple lighting. I'm starting to think these guys like the color purple. It looks retro and it has curtains to keep the area closed off.

I find the other office nestled in the back discreetly. "This is where we host meetings if necessary." This one is way bigger. It has an expensive-looking desk that is almost exactly the same as the one at home. *At home? Do I think of this place as my home now?*

There is a huge couch with two chairs to the side of it. There is also a decorative wall that's different from the one outside. This place is lined with black and purple too. The blend makes it look sophisticated and…is that a shower? I glance back at Ash, but he doesn't say anything about it.

So, I keep assessing the area when I catch a whiff of…

"Hey, Kitty Kat." Benji startles me from my thoughts when he comes strolling up to us in that laid back way he seems to carry himself in. "I forgot that I hate the whole shopping thing, so I decided to jump ship. Tyler is with them and will show them around." I internally chuckle, my kids can be a handful.

"Will there be music tonight?" I ask, hoping that there will be.

"There's always music playing, whether it be a DJ, a band, or Spotify. Today is Spotify." I try not to let my disappointment show. "Usually all the dancing happens on Thursdays through Sundays though. Why?" Benji asks, rubbing his smooth chin. "Do you like to dance?"

"I only went out before I met Theo. My friend Jess got us fake IDs and we'd go out dancing almost every day. But I haven't been since."

His lips get tight in irritation, but I'm sure it's not directed at me because he smiles once again. "Well, I can't wait for you to show me your dancing skills." He waggles his brows.

I don't think I have many dancing skills, but I love falling to the rhythm of music.

Ash's phone rings. He slides his hand to his front pocket and grabs his phone. "It looks like the kids are done and are ready to go." Sure enough, mine rings next, and I pull it out

MARKED WOLF

with a message from Ava saying they're ready to head back home.

"Come." Benji grabs my hand and we walk out together. I turn back to see Ash growling as he stares at our joined hands. I give him a cheeky grin just to piss him off and then walk down the stairs that lead directly to the bar. These VIPs have it good.

When we make it back to the truck my eyes nearly pop out of my sockets. The amount of stuff in the truck bed is insane. It's going to take me a whole year to pay this shit back.

"What the hell did you guys buy?" I stare at my kids as they look unashamed. All the bags and furniture give me anxiety. I didn't know they were going on a shopping spree.

"We need this stuff for our new rooms," Ezra says like they didn't just buy the whole goddamn store.

"It's true," Tyler agrees. All I can think of is how much this is going to cost me and how I'm going to repay them. "We've got it, don't worry about it." I look to Tyler. "Your eyebrows were scrunching really hard." I try to relax my face. These guys notice every detail about me. I need to get better at hiding my expressions.

"Shit, we've got to go." Ash purses his lips and rubs his eyebrows. The other guys tense up. "Benji, we can take the jeep and Kat and the kids can drive back to the house in the truck with Tyler."

This time I open the truck door myself, and the kids climb in the back. Benji and Ash waste no time taking off.

"Is everything okay?" I ask Tyler once we're on the road again. Looking outside, I still can't believe this is our new life. In a matter of twenty-four hours, our lives have completely changed.

"Yeah, I'm sure everything is fine." But I watch how hard

he grips the steering wheel. They're definitely hiding something from me. I'm just not sure what it is.

When we get to the beautiful mansion that I now call home, I get out of the truck and walk around the back to help unload. "We have people here that will take this up to their rooms." Sure enough, about five men come out of the house and start dragging in the comforters, clothing, and who knows what else my kids deemed necessary to buy.

"I'll be back soon," Tyler says as he jogs back to the garage and slides into a black Cadillac SUV with tinted windows and dark rims. I can't see his face, but I give him a small awkward wave. This is giving me hitman vibes.

I make my way to the house when my phone begins to ring, and I reach into my back pocket. My heart stops when I see who's on the other end of the call.

I walk to a bench overlooking a garden and sit down to take the call by myself. There is a pathway with roses leading up to a large fountain that's surrounded by decorative concrete.

My nerves get the best of me, and the suppressed feelings that I've been holding back today come rushing to the surface. My hands begin to shake. Maybe he wants to take me back, and if he does, I'd gladly come home. I'm ashamed to admit it, but it's the truth. Feeling nervous and hopeful, I swipe my finger across the green button.

"Hello," I answer. My voice is so soft to keep him from hearing the pain he's put me through.

"I'm having one of my colleagues draft up the papers for the divorce." My stomach sinks with dread. Not even a greeting. He goes straight for the punch in the gut. "It should be done by Friday. You can sign the papers on your way out."

This cuts deep. My throat has closed making it harder to breathe. Tears stream down my face. He has absolutely no intention of apologizing. It finally clicks, he's never going to want me again.

I want to fight back and try to see if we can work this out. I'll be better. I'll be whatever he wants me to be. I just don't want to feel alone anymore. I have an empty feeling in the pit of my stomach that I don't like, but I don't get to say a word because he hangs up the phone.

I stare at the roses and bring my legs up, resting my head on my knees and crying it out.

He doesn't even know or care that we're not at home anymore. He didn't ask about his kids or ask to talk to them.

What have I done to deserve this? I was always there for him and his career. I played the part of a good wife. I encouraged him to keep going for his Master's degree, always being supportive, and this is what I get.

I wanted so bad to be everything he wanted me to be, and I thought I was. Why is he treating me so badly? Or has he always treated me this way and I never realized it?

Exhausted with no more tears in my eyes, I wipe my face with my shirt and walk into the house pretending everything is fine.

CHAPTER 15

KAT

I nside the house, I walk by the office where I first met Ash. I open the door, surprised to find it unlocked. He probably forgot to lock it when we left to go eat lunch. I look around, making sure Ash isn't going to jump out of the shadows and attack me. When I'm sure no one but me is in here, I take my time eyeing everything.

Curiosity burns through me, and I have to see if I can find anything about the guys' business endeavors. Mostly to see if I'm right.

"What will you do if you find out you're right?" my wolf asks through a yawn.

I think about it for a moment. *"I have no fucking clue."* That's the truth.

I try to open the cabinet that's attached to the desk, but it's locked. I turn around to find more drawers but those are closed too. I was hoping to find something juicy to take my mind off my messy relationship, but I find something else instead. Something that has me focusing on that single item and nothing else. A black tie sits on the table, and I bring it up to my nose. There's a citrus and woodsy scent with notes of cedar and amber, which reminds me of pure sophistication.

Ash. I growl out.

I grab the tie and put it in my pocket. But not before I see something else sitting on the screen. Three words.

Violet eyes, why?

My blood turns cold. Is he looking into me? It is strange then that I have different eyes than them. Before I can look into it more, I hear a noise that startles me out of the office.

I climb up the stairs quickly, not wanting to get caught snooping. It's been a long day and I feel like a walking zombie.

Maybe I should ask them if I can start tomorrow instead of tonight. I don't think I will be pleasant enough to be around people right now, and I really don't want to be fired on my first day.

I store the "borrowed" tie next to my stash. I've moved it to my bedside drawer to be more discreet and lay down on the bed. My kids are too busy fixing up their rooms to see what's going on with me, which is probably a good thing. I don't want them to see me breaking down over their father.

I mope around for a few hours, but the scent of my borrowed items seems to really help comfort me. Maybe I should start taking their scents wherever I go. I have an over-sized purse that will make it easy to hide things. Except for the pillow, I don't know how to hide that. Unless I take the pillowcase off and take that with me, problem solved. If I need to calm down, I just grab an item and sniff it.

Fuck this is weird. Shifters are weird. I've officially lost it.

A little while later, there is a soft knock on the door. "Come in," I say in a shaky voice.

"I brought you dinner." Lily comes in with a tray of food

and sets it on a small table located next to the huge window that overlooks that gorgeous garden. "The kids are having their meals brought up too. They're busy decorating their rooms and the guys are currently out, so I figured you'd like to dine here instead."

I scowl thinking about Ash hanging out with Brooke. Lily looks worried when she sees my face. "But if you don't, I can bring the food back down. It's not a problem." Oh shoot, she thinks I'm annoyed with her. She's been nothing but kind to me.

"Oh sorry, I was thinking really hard. Please leave it here." She places the food down and turns around facing me.

"What happened?" she asks, obviously seeing my teary eyes and red nose.

I don't know Lily very well, she seems nice, but I don't trust her just yet. Especially after such a huge betrayal from Theo. I'm not sure how long it will be before I can trust again. "My husband is drafting up our divorce papers. I knew it was happening, but I also had a small hope that he'd come running back to me."

"Oh, I'm sorry sweetie," she says in a kind voice. "I know you don't really know me, but I'm a good listener."

"Thank you. But I'll be okay," I say politely, knowing that I'm not fine, but I don't really know where I am and who these people are.

She nods her head in understanding. "Call out from outside of your room if you need anything, I'll be able to hear you from the hall, just not from in this room."

"Why not from inside the room?" I say, lifting my eyebrows.

"The rooms in here are soundproof," she says, trying to hold in her laughter but failing because she cackles loudly.

"Why would they be soundproof?" I ask in confusion.

"Well…" She starts like she's preparing a big reveal, and it makes me even more curious. "When the guys used to bring women home, the whole house would be able to hear it," she explains carefully, like she's testing how deep my jealousy may run. I feel a pang of envy, then a small hint of anger toward myself. I have no right to feel so possessive toward the guys.

"Oh…" I try to laugh it off. "Okay, that makes sense." Wanting to get her out of the room quickly, I gloss over that bit of information. "Thank you for bringing me dinner."

She starts walking toward the door. "I'll pick it up a little later." She smiles again and closes the door behind her.

The plate on the table smells amazing. There's steak, shrimp, and a side salad. It all looks delicious. The pumpkin pie from earlier is on another smaller plate, but my body no longer wants the food. Instead, I feel nauseated.

I leave it for now and start getting dressed for work. There's no point in being here, all I'll do is mope around.

Someone put the clothes away while I was gone. So now I'm going through all the drawers trying to find where everything is.

I pull out some shorts and a low-cut top that's hanging in the closet. It's red and sparkly. I have no motivation to dress up, but I need to feel pretty for at least a night, and it's my first day on the job. I haven't had one in so long and I want to look decent and make a good first impression.

At the vanity table, I find a huge stash of expensive cosmetics that someone took the time to pick out for me. I have always loved going all out on my makeup; it's so relaxing and rewarding to create a work of art on my face.

But first I have to talk to my best friend. I know that she's worried, especially because I've been vague.

Me: I know I haven't called you back, but I will. I promise.

Jess: If I don't find out where you're living, I'm going to hire a PI.

I smile because, knowing her, she might actually do it.

Me: Sounds fair. I got a job working at a Lounge. Well, it's a club too. I start today.

Jess: WHAT!!!

Me: Yeah, and I'm so nervous. I haven't worked in so long. I hope I don't fuck this up.

Jess: Girl, you won't! They'll be happy they hired you. How did you get it anyway?

I bite my lip trying to figure out what to tell her.

Me: Soooo...

Jess: Yeah... Don't leave me hanging now.

Me: I'm living with four guys. Well one of them I haven't met yet. His name is Az. Benji is a rockstar god, Tyler is a sexy nerd, and Ash is well... he's an asshole. But they got me a job.

Jess: OMG! Please don't hold out on me. I want pics.

Me: That might be difficult.

Jess: Are they sexy?

Me: Hell yeah they are. I haven't met Az yet, but I'm assuming he might be too.

Jess: You've hit the jackpot and I'm so excited for you. Now go get ready for your first day on the job. Love ya.

Me: Love you too.

I put my phone down on the vanity table and start applying foundation over the redness around my nose. I apply extra concealer under my eyes to brighten them up more and add a smoky shadow of black and purple before going through the motions of blending it in. All my problems drift away at this moment, and all I'm focusing on is applying the right colors. Nothing in the world matters but creating the look I'm going for. I add a sparkle shadow on my lid and a highlighter to my brow to make them pop. After a thick coat of eye liner, I finish up with a rosy matte lipstick.

I look at myself in the full-length mirror hanging in the closet. "Not bad," I tell myself, walking downstairs in comfy black combat boots to wait for Benji. It's already dark, but there are lights surrounding the property. I sit outside overlooking the garden, taking off the coat that I brought with me.

It's always cold, rainy, and gloomy in Washington. Even though I've always needed to carry something to keep me warm at all times, it seems like I don't need it now. My body is regulating my temperature, keeping me not too cold and not too hot. This is perfect.

CHAPTER 16

KAT

A s I wait outside for Benji, I can't help the depressing thoughts that filter through my mind. I'm picturing Theo boxing up all my things and leaving them on the street for trash. I wonder if he'll leave the photos of the kids on the walls or if they truly don't matter to him at all.

Just as the tears threaten to fall again, I feel a rush of uncontrollable rage pulsing through me. There's my wolf. *"Calm down,"* I tell her.

"We should murder him. He didn't even think to ask how the kids were doing."

I don't have time to answer her before I see Benji pulling up beside me.

I'm starting to feel self-conscious as I make my way to the passenger side door. Maybe the makeup is too much for the first day of work. I should ask him to wait for me while I take some of it off. "Woah, Kitty Kat, you look so hot right now," he says as he steps from the car, his eyes drifting slowly up and down my body with appreciation.

"I should probably go change and take some of the

makeup off," I say as I turn around to make my way back to the house.

He scrunches his brows as he catches up with me. "What happened?"

"What…what do you mean?" I stutter.

"You've been crying." Oh shit, he can tell. I thought I did a great job covering the redness on my nose and the puffiness under my eyes. "No, your makeup is flawless. I couldn't see the tears, but your voice is another story. It's raspy and full of sadness."

I clear my throat. "It's nothing." I try walking away again but he holds me there with a stare so fierce I can feel it throughout my whole body. This is how I always wanted Theo to look at me, and maybe he did once, but it was a long time ago.

"It's not nothing." His voice is sharp. This is a side of him I've never seen before. He always seems so calm and cool, but right now he's neither of those things. "What happened?" I'm surprised when he uses his Alpha voice.

My wolf is intrigued and ready to submit to him. *"Weren't you pissed about this hours ago?"* I ask her. All she does is shrug, and I have to bite down on my lip to stay grounded and not give in. I have no idea what games she is trying to play, but she wanted to kill them yesterday and today, she's going soft for them.

I sigh tiredly. "Theo called and said he wants me to sign the divorce papers in four days and…I don't know," I put my head down in defeat. "I was hoping he'd want me back." I'm not sure why I just admitted that to him. I look back up knowing that he'd see the raw emotions swirling in my eyes. Regardless of how fierce my makeup looks; I know I can't hide the sadness I'm feeling in my heart.

He clenches his jaw before talking. "He has never

deserved you. You're better off without him." I give him a small smile. "You'll be happy here, I know it." He's so certain that it gives me hope. "Now let's get to work. I'm going to have to keep an extra eye on everyone at the lounge tonight." I give him a small smile as he tugs me back to his car and holds the door open for me.

As Benji gets into the driver's seat, I notice the intricate rose tattoos on his hands. It looks feminine, but he can definitely pull it off.

Benji is becoming a distraction that I welcome. I'm glad I decided not to skip out on my first day of work. "So, are you nervous about tonight?"

I think about it for a moment before answering. "Yeah, a little, but it does help to have a good-looking guy working with me tonight." I clamp my mouth shut. Shit. What did I just say? "I umm…" I stutter trying to come up with a good follow-up to my statement. "I meant to say that it would help if there was good cooking tonight. You know, so that there would be lots of customers tonight." I chuckle nervously. I want to facepalm myself, that made no sense.

"*Nice save.*" My wolf is talking to me like I'm an idiot.

"*Shut up.*" I bark back.

He snickers. "I'm glad you think I'm attractive because I think you're gorgeous." Heat creeps up my cheeks and my heart pounds so hard and fast that I know he can hear it. He doesn't mention it though, and I'm even more grateful for it. I would have died right here from embarrassment if he'd said something.

A moment later he says, "I'm the luckiest person alive right now. I can't wait for our date on Friday." I bite my lip. *See Ash, I think he does have feelings for me.* I wish he were here to witness this.

He pulls around to the back of the building when we

arrive. There are only six other cars here, so I assume this is where the employees park.

He gets out of the car, and before I can blink, he opens my door for me.

For the first time tonight, I realize Benji has changed clothes at some point. He's wearing a pair of torn-up jeans, high tops, and a band tee with a classic car and a man rocking a stand-up base on the front of it. "I like your shirt." He looks down.

"Thanks, I was looking for my favorite shirt but couldn't find it." I stand as still as a statue holding my breath. "Any idea of what might have happened to it, Kitty Kat?" he drawls.

I shrug. "No idea," I say in a rush and start walking toward the door. I hear him chuckle behind me before catching up.

He gently grabs my arm, and my body becomes alert from that small touch. We walk through the entrance and straight back to the kitchen area, where people rush around to get ready for the shift.

My stomach growls as the smell of the food hits me, and even though I skipped dinner, I couldn't possibly eat anything. It's not like I don't trust this place; I'm just feeling way too emotional to hold anything down at the moment.

"Hey, everyone." They all stop what they're doing to look at us, and I try not to shy away from their lingering eyes.

"Hi, Benji." A stocky man in a white chef's coat speaks up from where he's pulling items from the walk-in refrigerator.

"This is Kat, she'll be working the bar a couple nights a week. Kat, this is Joe, he's the head chef." Joe nods respect-fully as he continues to work. "This is Samantha, our waitress." He points to a slim woman with blonde curls sitting on the edge of an empty countertop.

"You can call me Sam."

"And Martin over there works at the bar." Benji points out a slightly taller man with brown hair and a friendly smile. Martin holds up two fingers in a silent greeting and Benji moves on. "Melissa here works at the bar too." He points to a brunette that looks freakishly similar to Sam, and I can't help but wonder if they are twins. "Steve and Tom are the cooks." Two younger kids in their early twenties are smiling up at me from where they lounge in a couple of barstools, their eyes wandering over me casually. I can't tell if they are checking me out or just super curious about who I am. Though they do look way too young for me, they're probably older than I am. I wonder when their aging slows down.

Once I've met the staff, Benji drags me out of the kitchen and back to the bar area. "Before I forget, there are other supernaturals that come in here from time to time."

My eyes widen. "There are more than just wolves out there?"

"Yeah, sometimes I forget that you just turned like yesterday and have no idea about the supernatural world."

"So, what else is there?" I ask, watching as he scours the bar shelf looking for something in particular.

"Well for starters, there are other shifters besides wolves." My mouth hangs open. "There are faeries and demons too. But if anyone tries to make a deal with you, make sure to come to me or one of the guys. Otherwise, you might accidentally be tricked into something you don't want to do." Closing my mouth, I make a mental note not to engage in any kind of dealings.

"That sounds horrifying." My wolf doesn't seem to think so. My wolf is somehow up for the challenge. I can't help but wonder if I got a defective one. She's going to have us both killed if she decides she can take them down.

"*The only one who's defective is you.*" I roll my eyes at her.

"It is horrifying. They can bring you back to their world and do whatever they wish with you." Damn, who would have thought that supernaturals actually exist.

"So how do I know if I come across them?" I feel unprepared for a job like this to say the least.

"Well, faeries look like humans but have pointed ears. Demons might be a little more of a challenge because they can have a variety of appearances. No two have the same skin color, eye color, or body shape. I'll be keeping an eye out to make sure you aren't blindsided," he reassures me.

"What about vampires?" I wonder if they can lure me in with their eyes like in the books I love to read.

"They are mostly harmless if you're supernatural. If you're human, that's when you'd need to worry." My kids should keep far away from here if it's where vampires might show up.

I realize that as much as I want to keep this from my kids, they're going to need to know enough to be prepared for a dangerous situation. I can't let them live in this world blindly.

"We'll start you off waitressing today, but I'll show you what we have for alcohol." I nod and follow his lead as he pulls a bottle of something I don't recognize from the top shelf. "It takes us a few drinks to get a buzz, so some people ask for faerie drops. And this." He grabs a blue bottle with a glass dropper. "Helps you get a buzz faster. You add about three drops to their drink." He closes the bottle. "We also have faerie wine." He points to the fanciest glass bottles that are lined up in the back. Those will get you fucked up, so you have to be careful how much you drink." After thirty minutes of him explaining what's on the wall and how to mix drinks, I go out on the floor to take customer's orders.

Benji is right at my heels, and I feel like his eyes are lingering way too long on my butt like I did with him earlier today. I don't mind him looking one bit, and I shamelessly sway my hips even more.

"Hello gentlemen, what can I get you?" I ask the two men sitting across from each other. The one to my right is wearing a red plaid button-up and the one to my left is wearing a blue one. They kind of remind me of lumberjacks.

Their eyes linger on my boobs way too long, and a low growl from Benji behind me has their eyes shooting back up to my face. They look startled. "Sorry Benji," they say in unison, bowing their heads in a submissive manner.

"What do I do?" I ask my wolf, hoping she'd know how we should approach this.

I can feel her stirring awake and yawning with a hint of annoyance. "*Nothing.*" Is all she says and goes back to sleep.

Well, she's no help. I'm not sure what to do, so I stand there awkwardly with a pen and paper in hand.

After an extremely long minute, Benji uses an authoritative tone to address the customers. "She's part of my pack and she isn't looking for a mate. You guys and everyone else will treat her with respect. Understood?"

"We will," the one in the red says, still facing the table.

"We didn't mean anything against you; it's only that my wolf got excited." Well, then maybe you should have looked at my face instead of my boobs, I think to myself. "It won't happen again."

"Don't apologize to me, apologize to Kat," he demands harshly.

"I'm sorry." They mumble together. I stay quiet because I

honestly don't know what to say. I guess there are bad apples in every species.

"You two may look up now and tell Kat what you want to eat." They both look at me and I fidget with the pen and notebook feeling uncomfortable. I hope it's not like this every night.

"I'll take a cheeseburger with tots," the one in blue says.

"I'll take a BBQ burger with garlic fries and a pitcher of bud." I write their orders down.

"Okay, I'll be back with that pitcher," I say, looking up from the pad in my hand. They don't make eye contact with me at all. Benji must have scared them.

I walk to the back and place the ticket in the holder strip. "I'm sorry if those guys made you uncomfortable," Benji whispers in my ear. My breath picks up having him this close to me. "Those guys are from another pack. We've got a hotel here for different species that want to hang out for a while. I'll make them leave. You just have to say the word."

I turn around and watch as his jaw twitches. I feel like he's more upset about this than I am. "That's okay, Benji. I'm fine." He watches me closely before nodding his head and going back to the bar.

He grabs a pitcher and fills it with beer, taking it to the table with the two men as I attend to other customers. I don't know if it's usually this busy, but I'm going to be on my feet all night. I go back to grab the two burgers from the first order, but Benji beats me to the tray.

"I'll take it this time." I smile at him gratefully. Although I avoid that table, I can feel the mens' eyes staring down my body and giving me goosebumps.

By the end of my shift, I am exhausted and excited at the same time. It was a busy night, at least for me. I haven't worked in so long, but I got about two hundred in tips and

I'm so excited. It feels so good to finally make my own money. I may not make enough yet, but this is a good start.

"You all can go ahead and leave. I'll lock up," Benji tells them, and I watch as they all gather their things and take off.

As the door closes behind the last employee, I start going through the motions of cleaning tables and putting everything away when Benji puts on a slow song. *At Last, by Etta James.* I look at him confused. "I wanted to do this earlier. I wasn't expecting people to stick around after we closed. I guess they were curious about you. You are rare, so I can't fault them for being curious." *Rare?* Probably because there hasn't been any one turned in a long time.

He grabs my arm gently, guiding me to the middle of the dance floor. His hands fall to my waist and I wrap my arms around his neck. His signature smirk is in place, taking my breath away.

As we sway back and forth, I stare at his emerald green eyes. My wolf peeks in for the first time and my vision changes. I'm assuming my eyes turn violet again because he gasps in surprise. Benji quickly composes himself, his own eyes changing to gold with flecks of green.

"Ow, what the fuck." I yell out in my head because my wolf has completely taken over and I have no idea what's going on outside my body. *"Let me out you bitch."* I yell at her, knowing that I called myself that name but not caring. I didn't even know she could do that. I know she's part of me, so all I have to do is figure out how she put me in this box. *Right?*

I look around frustrated by not being able to see an opening. I run my nails around the walls and they feel smooth on all sides. When that doesn't work, I pound with both fists. *"Let me out!"*

Think Kat, how do I get out of this box? I chew on my

fingernails, stressing out and wondering what the hell is going on outside my body. My wolf better not be doing anything embarrassing or stupid, but those are high standards to hold her to.

"That's it. I'm the one in control. I should be able to see if I want to." I push through my mind and find a block. Did I just purposely create this block letting my wolf take over?

I'm finally back at the bar and a look of recognition crosses Benji's eyes. "You're back. I thought I lost you there for a moment." His face relaxes as if he was worried when my eyes changed. Or maybe something happened when my wolf momentarily took over. Oh God, I hope not.

"Did anything happen?" I ask, but she doesn't answer me. *"Are you going to keep me in suspense?"*

"Maybe..." She drags the word along and I almost wish she were a physical being so that I could wring her neck until she answered me.

This wolf annoys the shit out of me.

After the music is done, I pull back from Benji, but he holds me close. I gaze up into his eyes and his look of want has my pussy throbbing with need.

I smell his male arousal and I'm sure he can smell mine too.

He puts his hand behind my head and pulls my forehead close to his lips. "Kitty Kat, I want you so fucking bad," he murmurs, titling my head upward and kissing the bottom of my lip. We break apart slightly. He's giving me some room to walk away but I don't want whatever this is to end. I want to be close to him. He looks at me like I'm the most precious thing in the world, and I didn't know how much I wanted that or how much I needed to feel wanted.

I have a need that only a man can help with. More than a

toy, it's the male connection I'm looking for, but not just with any guy. It's this man standing before me that I'm craving.

"I want this," I murmur. And that's the truth, I want it so badly. I want to be loved and cared for. I've had so many lonely nights and I'm not looking for more.

Hope and doubt fill his eyes, and I can tell he doesn't want to push me into anything. I stand on my toes and lean in to kiss him on the lips, showing him that without a doubt, he's exactly what I want. When our mouths meet, it's not soft and gentle the way I intended, but rough and desperate.

My back hits the bar table as he devours my lips, his hands blazing a fiery trail along my skin as he shoves aggressively at the hem of my shirt. I have no idea how we got here so quickly. His eyes dance in satisfaction as he rips my top over my head and trails his mouth over my collarbone, leaving goosebumps in his wake. He digs his fingers into my waistband and pushes my shorts and panties to the floor in one quick motion.

As I'm standing naked before him, Benji takes in a deep breath and pulls away to get a better look. Every insecurity I have about my body seems to flood back with his eyes on me. I think about my husband's assistant for a moment, of how I wish my body looked in the low light of the bar. He doesn't say a word, and I wish I could shrink away and cover myself to avoid any more embarrassment. A man like Benji could have any woman he wants; this was probably a mistake.

I raise my arms to cover myself, but a low growl slips from his lips as he looks me up and down, slowly taking in every inch of it, appreciating my body in a way Theo never did. Everything about him is pure male. It's giving me the confidence I need, and I don't feel like I have to hide anything from him anymore.

Everything about him screams to me, and I'm all in until I lower my eyes.

"N...no." I stammer, staring down at the monstrosity of a cock jutting out between us. "That's not happening, but this was fun while it lasted." I stumble back to gather my clothes from the floor when Benji slips his hand around my wrist carefully and pulls me back to him.

"Kat, eyes up here," he breathes, gripping my chin and tilting my mouth up. His lips move against mine at a tortuous speed, his tongue dancing over my bottom lip playfully.

"Don't worry about the size, shifters tend to be a little bigger than humans. I promise that I'll go easy on you."

I bite my lip, looking down at his body with every ounce of need I've suppressed for so many loveless years. He comes closer, coiling a strand of my dark hair around his fingers and searching my eyes for an answer. "We don't have to do anything you don't want." His sincerity melts my heart. It's clear that he cares deeply about me; I'm just not used to how sweet and attentive he's being.

"I want this, Benji." I thread my hands through his hair and plant a soft kiss on his lips, and my heart races as his hands trail down the small of my back. I'm tired of waiting for the divorce to happen. Theo doesn't want me, but the man before me does, and I want him too.

"So, just a heads up." He scratches his head, treading carefully. "When I'm close to coming, my dick will expand when I'm inside you." I have to do a double take from his shaft to his face, my mouth hanging wide open the entire time. I'm not going to lie, at the beginning, I was a little scared, but now I'm pretty excited about this. "I think you'll enjoy it," he says quickly, probably thinking I'll change my mind. "It'll hit your g spot and I will pounce on it over and over again and fill you up with so much pleasure." I gasp, wanting it more than anything right now. "But first I have to get you ready to take me," he says as he dips his fingers into my already wet cunt. "But it looks like you're already there," he whispers and my breath picks up. "Normally, I'd take my time and lick that sweet pussy of yours, but I can't wait. I want to be inside of you right now." His voice is raw with need.

If I wasn't already dripping, those words would have made me wet instantly. "Then what are you waiting for?" My voice is husky. I turn my body around facing the bar, giving him a view of my ass and looking at him over my shoulder.

"Fuck me, Benji," I say with a wink and turn my face around, lifting my butt in the air. He doesn't miss a beat. He pins me against the bar and rubs my cunt in small circles making me groan. I can feel that big dick on my back just waiting to be let in.

He thrust his finger in and out, my body going wild with need. "Please Benji, I need you." As if those words spark something in him, he lifts me higher and I curl my fingers on the edge of the bar, holding myself there.

He puts his head close to my ear. "You smell so fucking sweet, Kat. I can't wait to be inside of you." My nipples harden at his words.

He pushes into my entrance and I yelp. His head is huge. He grabs on to my breast while kissing my neck. I tilt my head back giving him more access.

He slips right in. "I'm halfway there, babe." *What the fuck, he's only halfway there?* I lick my lips in anticipation and excitement.

"What are you waiting for?" I ask breathlessly.

He pushes in further. "You're so fucking tight, Kitty Kat. Your walls are squeezing me. I need to stop for a moment before I come." His voice is strained. He pauses for a beat, regaining his control before thrusting deeper until I'm completely full.

"Benji," I moan, this new sensation is unlike anything I have felt before. Not even my toys can compare, and I've bought quite a few in different sizes.

"Wait till I fuck you and it expands, it's going to feel so good." Oh shit, better than this? I'm all for it.

And then it starts, and I howl with how intense it feels. My pussy constricts as he expands, hitting that sweet, sweet spot that he promised me. No one has ever done this to me before. "How does it feel, baby? Do you like it?" How does he expect me to answer with so much pleasure coursing through my body?

"Mmhmm," is the only thing I manage to get out.

This feels so good and so right, it's like I'm finally home. This is where I belong. Here with him.

He licks the back of my neck and I shudder as my walls squeeze him tighter and his thrusts become erratic. "I'm not going to last much longer." I don't get to say anything else when my release crashes like a freight train and he howls, pumping his seed into me.

He moves slower, emptying every last bit into me and my greedy pussy takes it all. He slowly slips out, and I'm already missing the feel of him in between my thighs.

"I'd say let's go for another round, but I need to take you home so you can get some sleep. You've had a long day and need your rest."

I still can't talk, so I only nod and he chuckles. With shaky legs, I pick up my clothing while he gets dressed too. I eye his dick one more time, licking my lips. I think I'm addicted.

"Kat, don't look at me like that or we won't make it home at all." Why do I secretly hope that will happen?

It's my turn to smile and we both quickly get dressed before we go at it a second time.

I walk back to one of the booths. "Let me go grab my purse." Taking it from the table, I walk back to the employee entrance and we leave together.

I'm surprised I'm not freezing to death. Normally I'd be cold and trying to run to the car or just avoid being out this late.

I grab my phone from my purse and quickly check to see if I might have any missed calls from the kids.

Seems to be good, they just said goodnight and that was it. I check to see if anything came from Theo, and I try not to let my good mood turn sour, but I can't help how much it hurts my heart.

"Fuck him." My wolf is aggravated that I'm still holding on to hope that he will come around. She's probably right, but we were together for so long that it's so hard to just let it go. I thought we had something. I invested so much time and energy into this family and into my marriage.

"Oh hey, it's nice to have you back in your cave," I say harshly, and I could have sworn she stuck out her tongue at me.

"You, ready?" Benji asks, holding the passenger door for me. I was arguing with my wolf and have no idea how long he's been standing there waiting for me.

I get up and sit on the seat. "Thanks," I say, looking around and trying to confirm that we are in fact back where we are supposed to be. Me in the outside world and her wherever she is in my mind.

"I'm always here, Kat." I roll my eyes at my wolf; she only comes out when she wants to.

CHAPTER 17

BENJI

When we get back home I go to my room, wishing I could take her with me. But I lay in bed by myself knowing she needs to get some sleep.

Kat looked damn sexy in her outfit. All I wanted to do all night was grab both hands and pin her against the wall near the bar and kiss her neck softly while I showed her just how much she affects me. Her scent, her body, and her wolf calls to mine, and I want to answer it. I'm so happy she wanted to share that moment with me. I don't think I could have waited until Friday to be with her.

My cock stands to attention when I think about her. I hope she notices how much she affects me, but more importantly, I want her to know that I'd never hurt her the way her soon to be ex has. She should be cherished.

I saw those violet eyes and it startled me at first. Ash told me about it, but I wasn't ready when I saw it for myself. A long time ago there were whispers of supernaturals with violet eyes but they became extinct, likely killed off. I never thought we'd actually see it.

I slowly put my hand in my pants, thinking of Kat's tight body and soft moans. I can't wait to see her on her knees, sucking and licking while I fist her hair and shove my cock down her throat until she begs me with her eyes to let her breathe. I want to hear her moan while she has it deep in her throat and watch her face as I explode into her mouth.

My body tightens, close to my release, when Ash walks into my room without knocking. I immediately pull my hand out and tuck my hardened dick in my pants, aggravated that he decided to walk in unannounced.

"How was her first day?" he asks with a smirk, clearly knowing what he interrupted. I bet he's jealous that I'm getting close to her. It's clear that he wants her, but he's still in mourning for what could have been, not that I blame him.

We all need to have our little fun to forget what was done to us, but I truly think this girl is different.

There's a ding on my phone and Ash growls as I open the message. He hates to be ignored.

Ava: Adding you now!

Me: Thanks!

Sitting back up on my bed, I smile and put my phone away. "We had an encounter with two dimwits at the bar tonight." I watch his eyes change color in anger the same way mine had. I nearly snapped their necks for staring at my girl like they had any right to her. "Calm down. I took care of it." I'm usually pretty laid back, but when someone I care about is disrespected, all bets are off. Kat hasn't seen the feral side of me yet, and I wonder how she'd react.

"She'll still want us." My wolf chimes in, and I completely agree. Even if Ash and Az decide to have a relationship with her, I know that she would want them too.

"I called the betas of the pack, Matt, Joseph, Carter, and Andrew, to handle the guys at the bar and scare them enough that they won't try it again."

"Good," is the only thing he says before changing the conversation. But, I know my brother well, and I know that he won't let this go. He'll probably go out there and hunt them himself. "I forgot to talk to Kat about the kid's school. I'll have to do that tomorrow. She probably doesn't want them to miss many more days." He rubs his temples, acting like it's a chore to talk to her, but I know deep down he feels something. I can hear the way his heart skips a beat when he talks about her.

"We've got to wait for her to tell her kids about supernaturals. Every single person in our school is supernatural." I feel bad that she has no choice, but if they're going to stay here, they'll eventually find out. There's no way to hide their new life.

"How do you think they'll take it?" The kids are down to earth, so they might actually think it's pretty awesome. At least, I hope so for Kat's sake. I know that she'd be devastated if they were afraid of her. She's been through so much already.

"I have no idea. It could go either way. But kids are usually more open to the supernatural world, and Kat took the news pretty well for an adult."

My eyes grow distant as I remember the way Kat looked at me on the dance floor tonight. "I was dancing with her and her eyes changed colors." He stills for a moment. I know Kat is special, but being special can get her killed in our world. I have to protect her from anyone that tries to take her away. The council hasn't called us yet, and I'm not sure what to make of it. She's been thrown into our world bitten, which makes her an automatic target, and now with her violet eyes, she'll surely be taken away from us.

"I'm looking into it," my brother says as he rubs his tired eyes. "I'll have you check out some places tomorrow and see if you can find anything about it." With that, he walks out of the room.

CHAPTER 18

KAT

It's Wednesday morning and I shower and dress quickly. I've decided today is going to be the day I tell my kids what I am. Just the thought of those words coming out of my mouth makes me want to hide in the closet and avoid them. But since I'm their mom, that's obviously not an option for me.

I hope they don't think of me differently. I'm hoping for the best, but it's hard not to imagine a bad outcome. This, after all, is not something humans would consider normal. Never in my wildest dreams would I consider this an everyday occurrence. But what happens if it freaks them out so much they want to move in with Theo? Would he take them back just to take them away from me?

Deciding to get this over with, I make my way downstairs. I'll make them breakfast and drop the bomb while they're eating. Since I haven't gone grocery shopping, I'll have to use the ingredients they have at hand. I thought I saw a grocery store on the way to the bar. I'll have to check later today to see if my debit card still works. If not, I have my tips from last night that I can use to pay for it. Thinking about the money I worked so hard for releases some of the tension I'm carrying.

Before I make it to the kitchen, I hear Ash's smooth tone vibrating through the walls, and I can't help but wonder what it would be like to wake up next to him, his low whispers setting me on fire. My body shivers, but I push the thought away quickly as if the boys would be able to read my mind the moment they see me. Ash is a dick, and I don't want anything to do with him.

"He should be back tonight. Az is at the cabin trying to extract the information from him. Benji, I'm going to have you go out there and help him out." It's looking more and more like they are assassins.

"On it," Benji says. I hear a chair screech against the floor before the door that leads outside opens and closes. There's a pang of disappointment when he leaves. I was excited to see him this morning. I'd trade Ash for Benji any day. At least Tyler will be here.

"There's food in here, Kat," Tyler says, surprising me. I stand up straighter, looking around to see if I spot any cameras. I do a 360 but find nothing. What the hell? How do they know? Are they spying on me somehow?

"You're loud, we don't need cameras to track you," Ash says. Well, that answers my question. I've got to learn how to walk quieter, and once I do, I'll scare the shit out of Ash just for being annoying as hell.

I push open the doors and walk right in. The smell of bacon, eggs, and pancakes fill the air, making my mouth water and my stomach grumble. I'm not much of a breakfast person, but Lily's food makes me want to eat.

"I have a plate for you already," Lily says, pointing to the mountain of food sitting on top of the bar in between Tyler and Ash. I try to school my face and show how grateful I am instead of the dread that's looming in the pit of my stomach. "You don't have to do that, Lily," I say, hoping that she takes the hint and doesn't try serving me again. At least when I'm in my room, I don't feel as guilty leaving the food behind like I did yesterday. The first night I thought she was dishing my plate as a welcome courtesy, but now I'm starting to think she does it all the time, and that's going to be a problem for me.

I have the urge to put it all back and serve myself. After all, I don't want to be wasting all that food. Right?

"Nonsense," she says, not realizing the internal debate that I'm having with myself isn't so internal. My breathing becomes quicker, but she doesn't seem to notice. "I'm going to let the kids know that they have breakfast ready." She walks out of the room, leaving me with both men and my mountain of food.

Tyler stands up and turns around to face me with a sexy smirk. My eyes wander down to his six-pack, making me briefly forget the negative voices in my head.

"You're staring at him because you haven't had the 'D' in a while. That wimp you called a husband could never satisfy you, but I'm sure any one of these men could, or maybe all four of them together," she murmurs, and I swear she winks at me for encouragement.

"I had sex with Benji last night."

"Yeah, and now you crave it more," she chuckles. *"You won't stop now that you've had it once."* My body freezes. Oh no, is my wolf right?

I don't pay my wolf any more attention because my full focus is on the man in front of me. His pants hang danger- ously low to his goods, and I bite my bottom lip hoping that maybe... I'm startled by a growl next to me. I look up at Tyler's face, but his arms are crossed and he's still grinning, showing me his perfect white teeth and those sexy as fuck dimples.

I glance across the table at Ash as he hunches over his food and eats like he didn't just make that threatening sound. "Come sit," Tyler says. "You must be starving."

I walk over and squeeze in between the chair and Tyler's half-naked body, and all I want to do is run my tongue down his six-pack. I stand in front of him and admire his caramel brown eyes and his sexy, pouty lips.

"Eat, Katarina," Ash says harshly, once again breaking the spell. "And step the fuck back Tyler so she can sit." Tyler doesn't seem fazed by his Alpha's tone, more like he's heard it so many times he's used to it.

"Hey, Mom," Ava greets me in a chipper mood as she walks into the kitchen.

"Everything smells so good, Lilly," Ezra says with eyes wide open looking at our breakfast.

As soon as she sets their plates in front of them they start stuffing their faces. "Wow! Why weren't you all this enthusiastic when I made food in the mornings? I recall making pancakes at least twice a week."

"Because you made us zucchini pancakes or coconut pancakes, never the real thing," my son says in between bites. I didn't even realize that I said that out loud.

They chuckle and I try to hide my hurt feelings. All I wanted to do was give them healthy foods. Especially since Theo was strict about not making any processed foods. I tried my best to provide the best of both worlds.

Lilly walks out of the kitchen and I figure it's now or never. My kids need to know what has happened, especially since they're going to start school here soon. They need to know what they're going to be dealing with.

My heart pounds erratically and there's a bead of sweat

trailing down my eyebrow. "Are you going to go for it?" Tyler whispers, clearly seeing my internal struggle.

"Yeah, I think so," I whisper back. He rubs my back in a smooth circle. My whole body tingles but it helps bring my anxiety down a notch.

I have no idea how my kids are going to take this situation. I hope they'll be able to trust me. I know if our positions were reversed, I'm ashamed to admit that I'd be slightly terrified and wouldn't believe them. Well, until I saw them shift, and even then, I don't think my mind would be able to wrap around the idea that they're a different species. I can say that if it had to happen to one of us, I'm glad it was me. I wouldn't be able to handle the anguish if it were one of them.

I look down at my untouched food, and before I lose my nerve, I spit it out. "I'm a wolf." Everything is so silent and both men stiffen. Ash raises his eyebrows, obviously surprised that I blurted it out so early in the morning. I guess I could have waited until we were all done eating and said it in a much calmer way.

Ava drops the fork and it echoes throughout the kitchen, making me want to cover my ears.

Shit, I should have waited. *"No, they'll come around, you'll see,"* my wolf says reassuringly. She's a lot more confident than I am.

"I don't know about that," I tell her. *"Look at their faces, they're horrified. I made a mistake. I should have waited."*

"Give them some time to process."

She's right, but it doesn't stop my hands from being clammy. I hate the waiting game, not knowing what they're thinking.

Tyler pulls his hand away to give me some space, but what he doesn't know is that his touch is the only thing that's keeping me grounded. It's almost as if my body craves the connection, but that's something to dissect another time.

Just when I'm on the verge of panicking, Ava smirks and slaps her brother's shoulder playfully. "Pay up."

Ezra rolls his eyes. "Shit. I knew I should have gone with wolf instead of vampire." My brows dip low watching this exchange, and I forget to scold him about his language. Did they not hear me?

Ezra opens his wallet and gives Ava a five-dollar bill. I'm still watching the exchange in confusion.

"Did you guys not hear what I just said? I'm a wolf," I say a little louder.

"Yeah, Mom." Ava goes back to eating. "We heard you loud and clear, you're a wolf now," she says, more interested in what she's putting in her mouth than finding out her mother is no longer human.

"Well…aren't you guys going to ask any questions?" I look at the other two men sitting next to me. Ash looks just as surprised as me and Tyler has the corner of his lip tipped up in a smirk.

"When did it happen?" Ava finally asks. I open my mouth to reply but she cuts me off. "No wait, I think I know it was on Monday. Probably when you went out to talk to aunt Jess."

"Yeah, you're right." I'm afraid to ask the following question, but I have to know. "Aren't you scared of me?" I look down at my food, not wanting to see their expressions. I know they act like they are fine with it, but I want to know the truth.

"Nope," they both say at the same time. I look back up, my mouth hanging slightly open in shock. Maybe they really are cool with it and perhaps Jess would be too. Nah, what am I thinking? She's an adult, and she'd freak out as much as I would. I wonder if I would be more intrigued about what happened to me if I were Ava's age.

I can hear my wolf cackle in the background and choose to ignore her sassy ass.

"Well, this went better than expected. They can start school today if you want," Ash says, typing away on his phone.

Both of my kids groan at the same time. "Can't we have one more day of freedom? You know, to adjust?" Ava asks as sweetly as she can with puppy dog eyes. I can't believe she still gets me with that look.

Ash looks at me, waiting on my decision. "Fine. But—" They both start cheering and high-fiving each other. "You two will go in tomorrow." I give them a pointed look, letting them know this is the only pass that they're getting.

"Since they're the new kids in town and everyone wants to meet them, I'm going to have a few of the boys come by today so they'll know some of the kids before tomorrow," Ash says, looking away from his phone and giving my kids a reassuring smile. I didn't know this asshole had it in him to be nice.

"That's a great idea." Probably the first time that I agree with this A hole. "Maybe knowing people will help them adjust at school." I hope my kids can find friends easily. Ava has always been able to talk to people, but Ezra has a difficult time trying to make and keep friends. Maybe it's all going to work out here.

As a kid, my life was constantly changing as I moved from home to home. There were dozens of new schools, and working up the courage to make new friends just to leave them behind was exhausting.

I was hoping to avoid that with the kids, but life didn't turn out that way.

"Did you know that we're wolves?" Tyler asks curiously.

"We knew that you guys were not normal." Tyler gasps and grabs his heart like he's been wounded by my son's words, but his grin says otherwise. "Not in a bad way. I mean, we knew that you guys weren't human." Ezra goes back to devouring what's left on his plate.

"So is everyone that lives here supernatural?" Ava asks, looking to Tyler and Ash for the answer.

"Yeah, our pack lives here and we occasionally get the other sups. You two will be attending 101 for supernaturals to give you guys a better idea of what other non-humans are out there." I should probably be taking that class too. I need to know what other creatures roam around, especially those Faeries and demons Benji mentioned last night.

My kids get up, rinse their dishes, and place them in the dishwasher. "You guys get ready, the other kids will be here soon," Ash tells them, putting his phone in his pocket.

They walk out of the kitchen, and as I stand to do the same, Ash clears his throat. "Where do you think you're going?" I look back at his piercing cold eyes. "Lilly said you didn't eat last night and you didn't eat at the club."

I grudgingly sit my ass down on the chair and begin to eat the eggs and bacon, but I stare at the pancakes like they're evil.

Ash grabs the syrup and nearly drowns my pancakes. Using a fork and knife, he brings a stack of fluffy pancakes to my face. I hesitate but open my mouth, and he shoves it right in as soon as my lips pull apart.

I close my eyes, savoring what I haven't had in years. I can see why my kids were stuffing their mouths. This is so much better than what I was making. I'd forgotten how delicious it tasted.

I moan over the fork full of heaven, but when I open my

eyes, Tyler and Ash are watching my mouth intently. I lick the syrup off my lips and it's as if they're mesmerized by the movement. Well, Tyler is, Ash schools his face and looks at me like I'm somehow offending him. I swallow hard and watch Tyler's dreamy gaze that should be reserved for the bedroom.

There's a knock on the door and they both look away from me, staring at each other in surprise.

Ash turns his agitated glare on me, like I'm the reason that someone was able to creep up on him. I'm assuming that nothing usually gets past these guys.

Tyler opens the door and a tall boy with bright blue eyes walks in. The moment my daughter emerges from the hallway, her light brown eyes lock onto the blue-eyed boy and my heart nearly plummets at their silent interaction. The rest of the group of kids fall in after him, but Ava pays them no attention.

No, no, no, this can't be happening. I want my daughter to focus on school and not have to worry about the complications that some punk kid in chucks will bring. In my experience, the more attractive the boy, the more trouble he causes. FUCK!

They keep staring at each other like none of us are here and it's only the two of them. The boy has a huge grin on his face that I'd love to wipe right off.

Tyler rubs my back to calm me. "That's Ryder." Shit, the kid even has a bad boy name. Ash sounds proud of him, and I wonder if he has potential to become an Alpha.

My inner wolf chuckles at my misery. *"Aren't you supposed to be on my side?"* I scold her. But, she's obviously noticing something that I'm not, or maybe I'm choosing to ignore whatever she's seeing.

They walk closer to each other and he sticks out his hand

for her to shake. "I'm Ava." She grabs it and they stare into each other's eyes.

"Let her hand go, now," Ash demands, but the boy growls, still staring at my daughter. I'm not so worried about him hurting her, I'm more worried about a relationship that will surely grow between them.

Ash stiffens, and before he tries to hurt the kid, I walk closer to him and extend my own hand. "Hi, I'm Katarina, but you can call me Kat. I'm Ava's mom." That seems to break the spell because he turns to me with reddened cheeks. He must have realized that everyone in the room was watching them.

"It's nice to meet you." He shakes my hand, not quite meeting my eyes.

"This is my son, Ezra." Ezra nods awkwardly but doesn't say anything.

"These are my friends," Ryder says with an authoritative tone, and I wonder if he's the leader of their group. "That's Tiffany." He points to a girl with curly, dark brown hair and green eyes. She gives us a small smile and a wave.

"This is Bryson." The boy he's pointing to has blond hair and blue eyes and wears a wide grin. Bryson reminds me of a California surfer, or at least what I would think one looks like. I haven't been to California yet, but I've always wanted to go.

"This is Zayden. We call him Zay for short." He points to the tall guy in the group with chestnut hair and a brow piercing over his stunning, topaz blue eyes. I've never seen that eye color before, and I know that my kids haven't either because we all stare shamelessly.

"You have pretty eyes," Ava says. He gives her a saucy smile as Ryder rumbles out a low growl.

"Calm down, Ryder," Tyler says in an authoritative voice.

So much Alpha energy is going on here. I wonder if meeting supernaturals always goes this way. If this is the way it works with kids, I can't imagine what it's like with adults.

"This is Cara." Tyler finishes the introductions. I look at her curly blonde hair and blue eyes, and she smiles at Ava. She's wearing a long, plaid flannel, a black crop top, and a high waisted skirt with tall boots. She envelopes my daughter into a hug, then Tiffany spreads her arms to hug them both. I can tell they're going to be great friends.

"I'm so happy to have another girl in our group. We were outnumbered but not anymore," she exclaims.

They break up their hug when another boy about Ezra's age comes in. He's wearing glasses and a long sleeve button-up with straight jeans and rain boots.

"I'm glad you came, Cash." Ash exhales in surprise.

"The others couldn't make it since they have a test today, but I'm here to show Ezra around." He looks at each of us shyly, his eyes lingering on Ava.

I look at my son and his shoulders relax. I think he might be relieved not to have to hang out with the kids that came in first.

"I'm Ezra, this is my mom Kat, and that's my sister Ava." Cash rocks back and forth on his heels nervously as I extend my hand in his direction. I can tell he's a bit of an introvert like Ezra.

"You guys have fun and show Ezra and Ava around to make them feel at home. They're part of the pack now," Tyler tells the kids, and I swallow through a thick lump in my throat thinking about those words and the life long commitment I signed up for.

Zayden quickly grabs my daughter's hand, and I watch as Ryder narrows his eyes on them. Maybe I was wrong, maybe Zayden is the bad boy after all.

Tiffany pulls Ava away from Zayden quickly with a smirk. "She's ours, Zay." The girls giggle as they walk out the door. Ezra and Cash are the last to leave.

Once the kids are out of sight, I yell out my most favorite word that I seem to be using quite often lately.

"Fuck!"

I know I can't stop her from dating, but I don't want her getting serious with a guy until she's at least twenty-one. I know that's wishful thinking, but the lingering thoughts of pregnancy come crawling back. It was never my intention to hold my daughter accountable for the mistakes I made at her age. She's different from me, and I know she won't make the same choices, but I still worry constantly.

Lilly startles me as she bounds back into the room. "If you guys are done, I need you out of my kitchen. I'm going to start on lunch." I grab my plate and throw the rest in the trash, feeling a little guilty about not eating more.

She tries to take my plate to wash it. "I can do it." I try to take it back when my phone rings.

"I've got it," she pulls the plate from my grip and smiles. I nod and let her do it because the name on the screen paralyzes me for a moment.

I look up at the two men watching me. Tyler has his brows downward in concern and Ash looks indifferent, but his eye slightly twitches, letting me know he's paying close attention to my movements.

Ash gets a phone call and frowns when he picks it up from the table. I don't stay to find out who it is because I have my own call to answer.

"I've got to take this," I tell them in a rush, practically sprinting to the door. My heart already feels like it's going to come out of my throat.

Once outside, I hurry down a path into the woods, hoping

the boys won't be able to hear my conversation all the way out here. "Hello," I answer, braced for an argument, but Theo takes a sharp breath.

"You…" he hesitates. "You're still alive?" He sounds surprised. Does he really think I'd die without his help?

I stand up straighter. "Why wouldn't I be? Do you honestly think I need you?" I say in a voice laced with anger. "I was fine by myself before you, and I'll be fine now. I think I can navigate life better as an adult." I snap back, only realizing that it's the first time I've stood up for myself.

"No reason," he says, confusing me further. "I'll bring the papers to the house on Friday."

I face the trees with a small smile on my face, the first smile I've had since the incident. "I've moved out." He doesn't need to know the details of how that happened, only that it did.

He clears his throat in shock. "Already?"

"Yeah, so if you want to move in with your assistant, the place is open." It hurts to imagine that woman in my bed or mulling through what's left of my personal belongings, but I keep my voice as calm and composed as possible.

"What about the kids? Where are they?"

As if he cares about them. Once upon a time, I did think he wanted to have a family with me, but I know better now. "Why do you care? They're out of your hair, that's all that matters to you."

He grunts. "Fine." After a few moments he asks, "Where are you staying?" I bite my lip nervously. The guys wouldn't want another man in their home, especially if he might bring trouble.

"I'll meet you at the diner to sign the papers." He knows which one; we've been there plenty of times. Maybe one of the guys can give me a ride or let me borrow a vehicle. They have so many I'm sure they won't mind. Although I have my eyes on that cherry red classic, I don't think they'd let me borrow that one, but it sure is a beauty.

"I'll have them ready on Friday." It sounds like he wants to say more. I bet it's killing him not knowing where we are. But I won't give him the satisfaction of telling him.

"See you then," I say with all the confidence I can muster, then I hang up before he can respond. My body is shaking with so much adrenaline. I can't believe how good it feels to stand up for myself. I should have done this a long time ago.

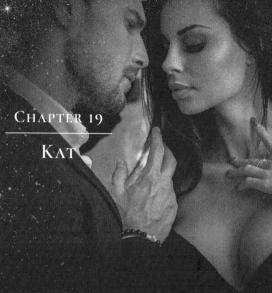

CHAPTER 19

KAT

Walking back into the house, my body is slowly coming down from the high of finally standing up for myself. I should have done this ages ago when I wanted to go back to school. I should have put my foot down and not let him dictate how I lived my life.

That's in the past now. It's time to focus on what's in front of me.

I walk in through the empty kitchen to find Lily digging through the pantry. "Do you need any help?"

"No, that's okay, but you can come sit and talk to me for a while." She grabs a bag of flour and closes the pantry door. "I like cooking, it relaxes me."

"I'm the same way with makeup." I make my way to the island and sit on the opposite side of her, watching as she measures ingredients and adds them to a glass bowl. "What are you making?" I ask, intrigued by the heavy smell of spices coming from the pot on the stove.

"I'm making fresh flour tortillas, and that is chile verde." She points to the stove. My mouth waters even though I just ate. "It won't be ready for another couple of hours."

"Where did you learn how to cook?" I ask, trying not to drool all over the counter after what she told me she's making. That's one dish I don't want to pass up.

She glances up with a faraway look about her, like she's reminiscing. "I lived in Mexico for a very long time. I used to travel a lot until I met two very kind ladies who took me in and taught me how to create authentic dishes." She has a longing look on her face and I wonder if they're no longer alive or if they were more than friends.

She doesn't continue the conversation, and I don't push her for more information. She gave me a glimpse into her past, and I'm grateful that she trusted me enough to share it with me. I hope that I can do the same when I'm ready to talk about my past.

There's a ping on my phone.

Tyler: Let's go, I'm waiting for you upfront.

Me: Okay.

"Tyler wants me to meet him outside," I tell her as I get up.

"You guys have fun." She winks and my cheeks turn pink.

Before I leave the kitchen, I turn back. "Thank you for sharing your past with me." She nods and smiles kindly as I walk out, heading straight out the front door.

Tyler is standing outside with a phone in his hand. "Yeah, that sounds like something's there. I'll look into it when I come back. Okay, talk to you later, Az." He puts his phone back in his pocket.

I wonder when I'll get to meet Az. I hope he's just as cool as Benji and Tyler.

Tyler's grin is so contagious that I can't help but smile back. My body relaxes, feeling lighter than I have in the last couple of days. Actually, if I'm being honest, I can't remember the last time I was able to relax before I came here.

As I stare at Tyler, I begin to hope that my life will get better from here on out. "Everything okay?" he asks casually, putting his hand in his pockets. There's a hint of worry lacing his tone.

"I'm meeting Theo at Sofie's Diner." He looks like he's trying to keep his composure, which is strange for me to see him this way. I know I haven't known him that long, but he seems so laid back. I would expect this from Ash but not from him. "I was hoping that I could borrow one of your cars, or maybe one of you could drive me there."

"Why didn't you just tell him to meet you here?"

"I was afraid he'd cause trouble. Besides, I have no clue where we are right now." I gesture to the forest that surrounds us.

I can't say that I hate this place. It's like a mini town, tucked away from the judgy eyes of my old neighbors. Everyone used to play nice with me because of Theo's status, but no one really liked me because I stood out like a sore thumb. I tainted their community just by existing a few shades darker than what they deemed acceptable.

They could practically smell the poverty I was raised in, and they acted like my very existence in their prissy neighborhood was going to bring their home values down.

"No," he says sternly, taking me by surprise. My wolf perks up wanting to bask in his tone. I keep my lips tightly shut so nothing comes out. She always stands to attention at the most inconvenient times. "I'm going to give you the address and he can come here."

I turn to him, eyes drawn in surprise. Not only by his tone but because he wants Theo to come here. "I don't think that's such a good idea, Tyler. He's not supernatural, what happens if he stumbles upon something that would freak him out? He'd try to get the kids away from me," I plead desperately. If Theo notices something is wrong, he'd use the dad card just to spite me. I never thought he'd want to do that, but now I'm finally starting to see who he really is.

"We won't let anything happen." He holds his hand to his heart in a promise.

I nod my head, not fully convinced but deciding to go with it for now. "Fine. I'll shoot him a text and let him know to meet us here. Are you sure that Ash will be fine with this?" I ask, still slightly skeptical. He's a control freak and no doubt would want to know about Theo coming here.

"Yes, it's fine. You know, I'm also an Alpha here, and I have authority, Kat," he bites out like I've just insulted him. I'm newly turned, and I still don't know their ways.

A flash of anger crosses his eyes briefly and they change to amber before quickly switching back to his chocolate brown color. "How did he draft up the papers so quickly?" he asks, looking out into the Wenatchee National Forest.

I shrug. "He might have been planning this for a while and had everything ready, plus he's a family lawyer and has always said that he has friends in high places. I'm sure one of them helped him out." While dragging my name through the mud no doubt.

He looks down to type something into his phone and I hear a ping from my pocket. I grab my phone and see an unknown number on the screen. "I just messaged you our address and everyone's phone numbers."

"When will I meet Az?" I question as I take the time to save everyone's numbers into my phone and send Theo the address of our new meeting place.

"He's on an assignment, but you'll meet him soon." I wonder what this mysterious guy is like. I always hear his deep, husky voice when the guys talk to him on the phone. He sounds sexy, and if he's anything like the men that already live here, I know he'll be a damn fine looking specimen.

Ah crap, keep it together, Kat.

"So where are we going?" We make our way to the jeep and I get in, taking a second to send a quick text to Ava and Ezra to make sure they're still fine

When they both reply quickly, I feel like I can breathe again. "I'm going to show you around the perimeter so you can get a feel of how big our land is." I look around at the beautiful greenery; this place is straight out of a fairy tale.

When Tyler stops, we get out of the car, and as the fresh, crisp air hits my nose, my wolf begs to run free.

"Come here." Tyler waves me toward him. "This," he touches a very thin, transparent material. "This place is warded against humans. They only come in if we want them to come in." I'm not sure where he's going with it, so I stay quiet. "If Theo tries to come again after this visit, we'll know. You don't have to worry about him trying to come back if you don't want him to. We only let the people we want come in."

That wasn't even a worry of mine. It was more like being afraid of him starting shit, but his reassurance makes my wolf really happy.

"So how do you guys ward it?" I ask curiously. "Do wolves have magic?" That would be so freaking awesome but scary at the same time.

"We have witches that have made this place their home too. They want to protect our land as much as the wolves do." Actually that makes more sense. I'd probably be terrible if I had magic. If I had to choose a supernatural being, it would have been a wolf. I may change my mind later if I find out dragons exist.

Something catches Tyler's eye and he goes outside of our safety net, stepping out of the shield that surrounds us. I try to do the same, but instead of letting me out as it did him, it keeps me on the other side.

I try to walk again before he comes back to stand next to me. "Don't worry about that," he chuckles, trying to play it off. My warning alarms go up and I try again. Blood drains from my face, and I feel like everything is closing in on me even though we're outside.

I look at him and start backing up. It's one thing to get me to join their pack; they never said anything about not being able to leave.

He stares at me with pleading eyes, begging me to trust him. He looks like he wants to say something, but nothing comes out. With every one of his steps toward me, I take a step back, distancing myself from him.

"I'm trapped." I say in disbelief.

My wolf gets angry too, and a growl comes out of my mouth. My body begins to shift and I'm no longer standing up with two human legs, but instead, I'm on all fours, growling at the man in front of me.

The shift wasn't bad like my first one. It surprises me and gives me hope that from here on out, my shifting won't be as gruesome as the first time. I turn to survey the area. In my wolf form, I can spot the border surrounding us clearly. I look back, and in Tyler's place, a brown wolf stares at me through amber eyes. He doesn't take another step toward me but keeps me in his sights.

With all the force I can muster, I back away from the invisible line that's currently holding me in. Tyler's wolf watches me closely, trying to figure out what I'm doing.

I pretend that I'm giving up, but when I'm far enough away from the shield, I make a run for it.

My legs are pumping, never losing sight of my goal. Tyler sees what I'm doing and he tries to catch up to me, but he's further away and won't make it in time.

I keep my eye on the target, and though I can almost taste freedom, it feels wrong that I want to escape this place. I don't know exactly what it is but something is telling me this is where I belong.

All I can do now is ignore it. I made my decision and keep running until I'm nearly there. I'm hoping that the impact will get me to the other side of this wall.

"Mom!" Ava screams and I immediately come to a dead stop, my paws sliding through the grassy field.

"*We can't leave.*" My wolf says in her most demanding tone I've heard. "*They're still here,*" she says softer.

Shit! She's right, we can't leave them here.

What was I going to do on the other side? I wasn't going to be able to help them. Who would I talk to? Who would believe me?

Everyone would think I'd lost my mind. I can just imagine how crazy I'd sound.

Hi officer, I just joined a pack of wolves because on Monday I got turned into one and now I'm one of the supernaturals. Then there's a wall that has been put in place by magic and I can't leave, but I still managed to break through. I know you can't see it, but it's there, and I need to get my kids out.

They'd probably send me to an asylum and then I'd never get my kids back.

I face Ava and look for Ezra, but he's not here. She comes running toward me. My heart flutters with happiness only briefly because the realization has dawned on me that she's running toward me, unafraid of my new form, with a blanket draped across her arms.

She comes close to me and gives me a hug. I try to talk but I can't form sentences with a muzzle. I turn back into a human, taking note that I am now fully naked. From now on, I should be aware that when I shift, my clothes shred. I should probably make sure I don't do that when I'm wearing really nice clothes.

She hands me the blanket as I whisper into her ear. "We're trapped."

"What are you talking about?" Ava asks skeptically. She's staring at me like I've lost my marbles.

"There is some type of border that's surrounding us," I say quietly, Watching as everyone else keeps their distance from us.

She scrunches her brows. "Where is the border?" Before I can say anything she gets up and runs, not knowing where it is because she isn't supernatural. She doesn't know that she's made it to the other side until she turns around.

"Mom! Mom!" she screams. Her face turns pale and her heartbeat picks up because she can't see us. So I guess it is true, humans don't know where this place is.

She crouches down on the ground sobbing, and the anguish in her voice has my body vibrating with the need to follow her. Before I can try to get to her, there's a figure that runs past me with lightning speed, flying through the border effortlessly.

Ryder picks up Ava, whispering in her ear and trying to calm her. He holds her against his chest while she clings tightly to him as if he might disappear. He walks back to us carrying her the whole way.

"I'm sorry, Ava," I say, feeling guilty as I hold on tighter to the blanket that covers my body. She looks at me briefly and nods her head.

She had no idea that she wasn't going to be able to see the

barrier that divides this place from the outside world. I didn't warn her and she was unprepared.

Tyler comes up to me and hands me his shirt. I have the urge to rub it against my face but fight against it as I immediately put it on. I'm grateful that he gave me something to cover up with, but I'm still confused and angry as to why I can't leave this place.

"Thank you for coming, Ava." That son of a bitch used my daughter to keep me here. I assume that he's the one that called them hoping Ava would be able to calm me down. "And sorry about that. Ryder, why don't you take Ava shopping, it's on us," Tyler tells him, and I let them go because it's obvious that my kids are free to go whenever they want. For some reason, I am the only one that seems to be stuck here.

They get into a black car, and I watch them disappear as Ava waves to me from the window. I'll have to talk to her later and make sure she's truly fine, though I know buying clothes will sweeten the deal.

He turns back to look at me. "I'll get someone to mark the whole perimeter so that doesn't happen again." And I know it's for Ava and Ezra's benefit, so they don't accidentally walk out of here and get stuck on the wrong side.

"Can she leave because she's human?" I finally look at his chocolate brown eyes again.

He rubs his chin for a moment before answering. "No." I wait for him to explain further but he doesn't offer more.

"Then why was she able to leave?"

"Because she can." He won't look me in the eye, something is wrong with this.

"Well, why can't I?" I stand up from the ground and cross my arms over my chest.

He's rubbing his forehead, clearly debating what to tell me, when we see another car pulling up.

Ash. Oh great, just what I need, another cryptic asshole.

He gets out of the car wearing a black suit. Apparently, that's his signature look. It's what I've seen him wear for the past couple of days. He reminds me of Johnny Cash, and even his sunglasses are black.

He walks to the front of the car with an air of authority that sparks a need deep in my belly. Apparently, my vagina and wolf are working together because I can't stop wondering what he looks like under that suit of his. Is he as dark in bed as his clothing portrays him to be?

Ah fuck, here we go again, focus Kat. You're trapped here. "I felt Ava leave the perimeter." He ignores my whole existence, only talking to Tyler.

"She's back inside the border and safe with Ryder." Tyler explains briefly.

Ash nods his head. "And I felt her trying to leave," he says, staring all the way into my soul. My body shivers under his brash tone.

He looks down, just noticing what I'm wearing, and there's a low grumble in the back of his throat. I tighten the blanket around me even though I'm still wearing Tyler's shirt, which pretty much covers me up to my knees. But Ash makes me feel as if I'm naked.

"Why can't I leave?" The sharp tone in my voice surprises me. I didn't mean to sound so harsh, or maybe I did. I'm pretty pissed off right now.

He grabs a pack of cigarettes and a zippo like we have all the time in the world. He lights one up and inhales deeply, letting the smoke trail from his lips slowly.

I've personally never smoked before and have never wanted to try it. It's a bad habit, but damn if Ash doesn't it make it look sexy as he leans against the hood of his car looking so relaxed and composed.

Tyler leans against a tree as if he knows that this is going to take a while. We all stand in silence while he finishes his cigarette, and just when I get excited for the answers he's about to give me, he lights up another one. I groan. Are you fucking kidding me?

"Ash?" I shout, but he doesn't answer, and when he finally looks at me again, it's like he doesn't have a care in the world. I hate this guy more and more every day.

My patience is running thin, and I'm about to snap again when he starts talking. "I had a witch ward it to keep you from leaving." My jaw drops. I already knew about the witches, but not about the part that keeps me here.

"I told you this was going to backfire," Tyler hisses, resting his back on the tree. Ash ignores him.

"Okay, I got that part." I let go of the blanket, putting my hands on my hips. "But why?" I'm starting to understand why Tyler wanted Theo to come here; they didn't want me to leave. They were probably hoping I wouldn't find out.

"Because you have a huge target on your back right now." All I can do is gasp because I know that there is so much more to this that he's not telling me.

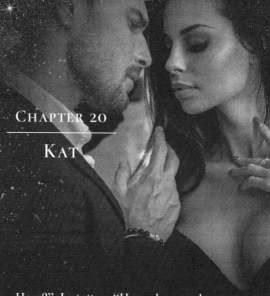

"What… How?" I stutter. "How do you know that?"

"He's looking for you," he chuckles darkly, ignoring my question. "And he's pretty pissed about you stabbing him in the eye from what I hear." He finally takes his glasses off. "How did you manage to stab him while in pain?"

Ash's blue-green eyes search mine for answers. "So you knew who attacked me and withheld the information?" My vision starts changing, and I watch as his eyes flicker to a shade of gold.

"No, I found out this morning. I got a call during breakfast." Oh, that's why he looked concerned. "Does the name Dante sound familiar?"

I run through the list of people that I've met most recently, but it doesn't take long. "No, I have no clue who it could be." I wonder if I was being watched this whole time and never noticed. I lived in a nice neighborhood, even though I didn't fit in. Neighbors would report suspicious activities and we had a cop drive through our streets every couple of hours. I didn't have to watch my back like I did when I was younger.

My vision goes back to normal, but Ash's stays the same. I almost want to turn around from his deep gaze, but I hold it together and stare right back. I would have never done this as a human. I'd look away first or look down, and for some reason, that makes me angrier and gives me the desire to hold it. I can't help but feel this is a test of some sort, but I have no clue what it could be.

"Come on," Tyler says from right behind me. "Let's go get you some clothes." As I'm being dragged back to the car we glare at each other, none of us losing eye contact. Ash smirks and that's the last I see before I'm pulled away.

I wait until he's seated in the car to tell him. "I'm so mad at you, Tyler." I cross my arms angrily, looking away from him and watching the trees as we drive. "You shouldn't have used my daughter against me."

He sighs deeply like he's in pain, but I'm too annoyed to care. "Sorry Kat, but you lost it there for a minute. You went feral and I didn't want to hurt you. I figured if you saw one of your kids, you'd calm down." He rubs his brows. "It wasn't my plan for this to happen. I wanted to show you around and show you how special this place is." This place is absolutely gorgeous, but I don't want to tell him that I'm still feeling a little salty about it.

"Why did you go out, Tyler?" I watch for his reaction, but he keeps his face perfectly schooled. "What did you see out there?"

"We're afraid that the person who turned you is going to try and take you. I thought I saw something moving in the shadows, but I couldn't really tell." He takes a deep breath. "Kat, we need to protect you at all costs, and that means we have to also protect you from the person who turned you." I don't know what to say to that, so I stay quiet the whole drive home.

At home, Tyler tells me he has stuff he needs to do and my kids are at the movies with their new friends. Apparently, they also have a movie theater here, so they won't be back for a while.

I grab a salad for lunch that Lily offers me and bring it upstairs to eat. Once I settle into my vanity seat with my salad, I look at my phone, noticing I have calls and messages from Theo's best friend, Dan.

When I'm done eating, I decide to put him at ease, hoping he truly has my best interest at heart. I message him back telling him that the kids and I are okay. I also let him know that I'm not in the mood to talk over the phone just in case he's phishing for information for Theo's case. I keep that last part to myself. My text seems to calm him down a bit because he just says he misses me and we'll talk later.

An hour before I leave for the Crescent Lounge, Lily brings in more food and my stomach growls, remembering the spices from this morning. "I know you were wanting some of this before you left." My greedy eyes follow the tray to the table where she places it, and I nearly jump out of my bed to get to the hearty plate of food. "This dish always goes quickly, so I wanted to make sure you eat before you leave since none of the guys are here yet."

"I've been waiting for this all damn day, the smell has been taunting me," I say as I sit at the table. She giggles before she leaves the room.

A few bites in and I'm nearly done. I can't believe how good fresh tortillas are. So much better than store bought ones. After this, I don't think I can ever go back to buying them.

Once I'm done, I get dressed quickly. I had put on makeup before the food came, so all I had to do was get dressed. I'm wearing a lace sleeved V neck with black, high waisted pants and knee-high boots.

Tyler has really good taste in clothes. I would have never picked this out for myself. It's giving me witchy vibes, and I love it.

I message both of the kids in our group chat.

> Me: Hey I'll be heading out to work soon. Don't come home late, remember you've got your first day of school tomorrow.

> Ava: We'll be home in an hour. Be safe
> Love ya.

> Ezra: Love you mom.

> Me: Love you both.

> Benji: I'll be outside in five minutes

I scrunch my eyebrows together. What the hell? Who added him to the family chat?

> Ava: Hey mom hope it's okay that I added Benji

She sends it to me privately.

> Me: Yeah sure, that's fine.

I switch back to the family chat.

> Me: Ok I'll be there soon.

I get my tray and leave my room. I could really go for some seconds and the thought surprises me. I've never gone back for seconds. But there isn't enough time, I need to get to work and make that money.

I grab a Tupperware bowl and add some of the food with a side of tortilla, then find a grocery bag from the pantry and tie the food up securely before putting it in my oversized purse and leaving the kitchen.

Outside, Benji's flirty grin greets me, and I can't say that I hate it. I walk to the passenger side of his car and get in. "Hey there, Kitty Kat," he drawls, and I tighten my thighs together hoping he doesn't notice or smell the liquid pool between my legs. If he notices, he doesn't say anything. Thank God, I'm already mortified by how my body reacts to them. "Did Lily make chile verde? I can smell it all over you." I nod, "Fuck, I know there won't be any left for me before those assholes devour it," he whines.

I chuckle before pulling the bag out with the yummy goodness he wasn't expecting. "You're in luck Benji because I sneaked some out for you." I didn't know if he had eaten already but Lily had said that all the men here liked it and I knew there wasn't going to be any left. I wanted to make sure Benji got some too.

"Yes!" He shouts excitedly, "You, Kitty Kat, are my favorite person," he says before kissing me on the cheek, which makes my wolf excited.

At the Crescent Lounge, I get to work. Benji shows me what I need to know behind the bar, and I get lost to the rhythm of making drinks. I'm surprised how fast I'm getting the hang of this. I thought for sure it would take me months to learn how to mix drinks. It helps that I'm never by myself at the bar and can always ask questions if I need help.

Two beautiful ladies come up to the bar. The one on the

right has a very pale complexion with long white hair and clear, white eyes, and the one on the left is the complete opposite with a dark complexion and hair darker than mine. I didn't think such a color could exist, but I'm staring right at it.

They look to be twenty-five, but who knows, if they're supernatural, they could be ancient.

"Child, come here." Well if that's any indication, they're indeed older than me. When I step in front of them, their eyes are old and my body shivers when I stare into their knowing depths. They look deep into my eyes like they're extracting all my secrets. But that isn't possible, or is it? Are they fucking demons? Maybe I should call Benji to help me out. I desperately look around the seating area, hoping to catch a glimpse of his red hair. Shit, he's probably eating in the kitchen.

"Relax girl." I snap my attention back to the one on the right, the one whose hair is white as snow. "My name is Althea and my sister's name is Imani." Her voice sounds old and raspy. I wouldn't have been able to pick up on it as a human, but as a wolf, I can hear tones differently. "We just want to meet you, Kat. We mean no harm." My body stills. It's what Ash and Tyler had mentioned earlier, but why. "It's a shame that it had to fall on you. Especially because you have kids." What the hell are they talking about? The air around us seems to change as my breathing slows. It's like no one else is here but the three of us. Where the fuck is Benji? My breath starts to pick up.

"Yes indeed, what a shame. Who will take care of them when you're gone?" The other sister sighs, her eyebrows scrunch together and they face each other in sadness. I'm confused about what's going on right now. Are they telling me that I'm going to die? I really hope not, but it's not looking too good for me.

I swallow hard before she starts talking again. "Tell me, Katarina…" She comes closer, licking her lips. "Are your eyes violet?" My heart is pounding so hard that I'm surprised it hasn't made a hole through my chest. "Do you know who your parents are?" My hands get clammy. Why do I feel like they know more about my life than I do?

Before Imani can open her mouth to speak, Benji's stern voice cuts her off. "What are you two telling my dear friend, Kitty Kat." He still wears an easy smile, so I can tell he doesn't feel threatened by the women. I'm starting to think he wears a shield to hide what's really underneath his carefree persona.

"Have you heard about the curse?" My eyes open wide, but Benji doesn't look surprised at all. Clearly he knows something and they're keeping it from me.

"Enough," Benji shouts, startling me and a few others that were sitting around us. They only smile mischievously like he doesn't scare them.

"You best be careful girl. This new world of yours is not for the faint of heart." My hands twitch slightly at her words. "Watch your back." There's a sudden blur, and before I can react, Althea grabs my hand so fast. How was she able to move so quickly? Benji pulls them away from me, but not before something is placed in my hand. Benji is shouting at them, but my mind is on the object that's in my hand. They look unfazed by Benji. "For you," she says. "A gift." They get up and leave while I slide the metal piece into my pocket.

I'm still staring at the door long after they're gone when Benji gets right in front of me. "Kitty Kat, look at me." I drag my eyes away from the door and look at the man before me. "Are you okay?"

It takes me a while to respond. "Yeah, I'm good. Who were they?"

"Just some crazy supernaturals that like to spew nonsense." Somehow that doesn't seem right. I think he's saying that to avoid the conversation about the curse. Who's cursed? Is it me because I became a shifter? And what is hanging in my back pocket?

He never saw what they gave me, and because I don't want him to ask any questions, I make my way to the other customers, leaving him behind.

The rest of the night goes by rather uneventfully, but I have that piece of metal burning a hole through my pocket. I can't wait to go home and see what the hell it is and what I've gotten myself into now.

CHAPTER 21

TYLER

I hate what I did to Kat earlier today. I would have stayed with her and begged for her forgiveness, but I had to get some work done. If it wasn't about her safety, then I'd worry about this later, but we need answers now.

The day was going so great until I saw someone out by the perimeter. That's why I needed to go and check my cameras but didn't want to scare her too much. We have to be alert to make sure there aren't any threats.

I message Ash.

> **Me:** There was someone out there

> **Ash:** Can you tell who it was?

> **Me:** No it was just a shadow.

> **Ash:** I went out there after you two left and couldn't catch any smells.

> **Me:** Yeah I didn't either that's why I found it strange but there was definitely someone out there.

Me: I'll let you know if I find anything else.

After I've exhausted all avenues trying to figure out who might have been lingering outside, I go and try to research more about Kat.

I make sure I do this part discreetly. We don't want more people finding out about her. I'm the best we have at hacking and hiding my tracks, but after a while of researching and hitting wall after wall of sealed foster care reports, I'm starting to doubt my skills.

I may be able to ask her about her past, but she didn't even know this world existed before she was turned. It's doubtful that she would recognize any connections she has to our world.

When I can't seem to get anywhere, I decide to go for a run in my wolf form to curb my frustrations. We've got a big place here, so we don't usually have to worry about intruders and hunters. People can't cross our property, but the shadow on the security camera still lingers in the back of my mind.

Ditching my clothes on the porch, I shift into wolf form, feeling the immense power coursing through my limbs. The crisp air tousles my fur as I take off toward the forest, right back to the edge of our property where I'd seen the intruder earlier. Humans can't get past our magical barrier, so it could have been a random hiker passing through. But I have to be sure.

Nothing looks or smells out of the ordinary, but having Kat here has made me paranoid. If two random women at the bar ventured out to see the infamous violet-eyed wolf, surely the council has heard about her as well. They could be watching from afar, waiting for their opportunity to take her away from us.

I finish running the full perimeter and head home, turning into my human form the moment I hit the porch steps. Pulling on my jeans quickly, I head back into the house to get to work.

Chapter 22

I 've been tossing and turning all night, wondering if what the sisters said is true. I put the cool metal stick they'd given me in one of my drawers after fiddling with it for hours. I have no idea what it is or what it does. Maybe I'll just ask the guys tomorrow and see if anyone knows.

Feeling restless, I look at the clock on my nightstand. It's midnight and the house is quiet, but maybe walking around the house a bit will do me some good.

I open my bedroom door and peek outside to see if anyone else is roaming around. Finding the halls vacant, I try to stay as silent as possible so I won't wake anyone up.

The hallway is dimly lit by sconces hanging from the walls, casting long shadows over the hardwood floors. During the day, this mansion is overwhelming, but it's more than that at night. Thank God there are no creepy portraits hanging on the walls. I don't think I'd ever leave my room if there were.

I make my way downstairs, walking light as a feather, or so I hope. According to Ash, you can hear my heavy footsteps, so I'm trying my hardest to be silent.

I surprise myself when I walk into the kitchen area. It has never really been my go to. I decide to keep the lights off. If I need more light I can change my eyesight. My wolf can see better at night. The large stainless steel fridge that practically takes up a whole wall is right in front of me. What am I doing? I shouldn't be eating this late. I'm going to gain weight. Painful thoughts from the past come crashing back to me. I try to push down the nagging belief I shouldn't eat past six. That idea has been ingrained in me since I met Theo.

"Kat, you shouldn't eat that. It already looks like you're gaining weight," he says, sitting down at our kitchen table. He's staring at his phone intently. I didn't think he'd notice me walking past him to the fridge carrying Ava in one arm. He's been ignoring me all day and just now he decides to pay attention to me.

"But I'm still hungry, Theo. Am I not supposed to eat?" I laugh nervously meaning it as a joke, but when I look at him, he shrugs, still not making eye contact. Obviously his phone is more important than talking to me.

Feeling guilty, I put the food back in the fridge and go to bed starving. I barely had anything to eat all day because Ava needed my full attention. When I lived in foster homes I was lucky if I got dinner. I usually ate at school, but now I have the means to eat and I get shamed for it.

Not wanting to lose my nerve, I push those thoughts away and open the refrigerator. The blinding light greets me and I shield my eyes as I move food around on the shelves. Lily was right, there is absolutely no chile verde left. I'm glad I packed some up for Benji. My heart flutters when I think about how excited he got when he saw the food.

I spot the pie from a couple of nights ago that I didn't eat. My mind briefly goes to my weight again. It's a challenge to force myself to go for it. Those lingering thoughts come crashing down, but I fight them, and before I have time to dwell on this, I grab the pie and some whip cream. I close the door and yelp, nearly dropping the sugary sweetness.

Hiding in the shadows is a man. He has his arms crossed in a menacing posture and he's tracked in blood across the floor. I was so focused on my battle with eating that I didn't notice the change in scent.

"Who are you?" My voice is soft and low, but I know he can hear me. He doesn't answer, only stares, tilting his head in an animalistic way. Like a wolf watching its prey. Nothing about his gesture is human.

This man doesn't have to tell me who he is because I know exactly who's standing there being all creepy and shit. I can smell his scent lingering in the air, the same scent that lingers in my bedroom because I stole—I mean borrowed —from him.

Feeling kind of awkward, I almost want to put the dessert back and run to my room, but I don't want to give him the satisfaction of leaving. Plus, I worked hard trying to over-come my fears.

Instead of running off, I grab a paper plate from the pantry and bring everything back to the bar. My body shivers as his eyes follow my every move. I cut myself a slice and add whip cream. The sound is so loud against the quiet surrounding us.

Don't be afraid to eat this. Don't be afraid to eat this. I keep telling myself over and over when the anxiety comes creeping back.

When I've finally calmed myself, I look up to see him standing on the opposite side of the bar and nearly drop the fork.

The bright moon shining through the window lights up his face, and I notice his features better now. Those dark blue eyes assess me the same way I'm analyzing him. The first thing that I spot is the tattoo just above his eyebrow that says Iron Beast with a teardrop just below his eye. The inside of his lip has a bright red tint to it. His sandy blonde hair is cut short with blood running through it.

The way he's dressed is a total contrast from what I expected. Instead of all black like Ash, he has a dark suit with a red satin shirt and a red handkerchief displayed in his chest pocket. He is drool worthy, just like the other men in the house.

There's a silent loathing that radiates from him. He's looking at me like he wants to rip my head off.

My wolf perks up as soon as she catches his scent. She wants to rub all over him and bask in the familiar, calming smell.

"Are you going to just stand there and watch me eat?" I ask as I slide my fork into the slice of pie. I try not to moan at how good it tastes when it hits my mouth. I don't think I've had something so sweet and delicious my whole life. He watches my lips in fascination before he catches himself and clears his throat.

He lets out a startling growl. "I don't like you." His voice is low and husky but authoritative.

He's nothing like Benji or Tyler's playfulness and nothing like Ash's seriousness, he's…his own breed.

Ash was wearing a scowl when I first met him. This guy looks at me like I'm a fucking disease.

I decide to be friendly to see if it helps any. Maybe he's super shy and needs encouragement. "Look, Aziel, I didn't want to be a wolf and I sure as shit didn't want to stay here, but this is what happened and we both need to live with it."

"First off, don't call me Aziel," he snaps. Now that I think of it I only heard his name once and the rest of the time they've called him Az. I guess he doesn't like his name. "Second, I know you took my pillow and you can keep it," he says accusingly. I try to keep my face neutral and give nothing away, but we both know I definitely took it. "I don't want your lingering scent on my things" Okay ouch. "And third, stay out of my way," he says as he storms off, and I'm assuming it's to go take a shower, or at least I hope it is because he's drenched in blood.

My wolf sees this situation as a challenge and jumps up and down with excitement.

I finally get to enjoy the rest of my pie, but my mind wanders back to my encounter with Az. When I'm finished, I put everything back in the fridge and throw my plate and fork in the trash and go back to bed.

This time though, my heart is feeling content with the little slice of heaven that I just had, and I go right to sleep.

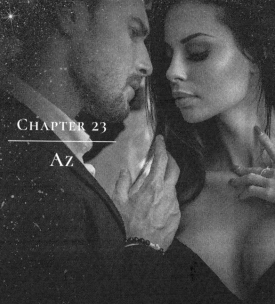

CHAPTER 23

AZ

She needs to go.

I have a feeling she's going to break through our tight bond, and I don't like it one bit. I know that we need to keep her safe according to Amara, but I don't understand why the weight of her fate is on our shoulders. We've already had so much shit to deal with, we don't need to babysit her and her kids.

Her sweet cherries and citrus scent is alluring and wakes the beast within me, but I've never been in a relationship before. I don't like the attachment that it brings. The chance of being with someone was taken from us, so I don't care to try and entertain the idea. I only fuck, and that helps keep my head clear.

Kat looks like she'd become too attached. Or maybe not, maybe she'd be perfect. She's getting out of a relationship and probably doesn't want another one so soon. Maybe I should try to get in her bed.

If she wants a relationship she can have one with Benji or Tyler, I'm sure one, if not both of them, will want to be her boyfriend, or whatever relationships are called these days.

"She can be underneath us all tied and gagged at our mercy." My wolf is on to something. My cock springs to life. Her in my bed with her hair splayed out. Tied up in my favorite color red, the color of blood. I can't wait to see what she looks like in red. I bet it would be utterly sinful. I bite my lip hard just thinking about it. Her legs wide open, giving me access to her slutty cunt. I bet she tastes as good as she looks. Her husband is a fucking idiot for getting rid of her, his loss.

I can see it now, stroking myself up and down as she stares at me from the bed, struggling against her binds with her pretty brown nipples on display for me to bite and suck. She'll lay there and take what I give her. My cock throbs achingly, and my wolf howls.

I stop my lingering thoughts before they get any further. I need to talk to my brothers and ask for updates, but I really don't want to see Ash right now. He's going to grill me with questions. So instead, I go to meet Tyler. I bet he's in his room doing tech stuff. I honestly don't know how he gets the information he needs. I tried it once and got so frustrated that I yanked all the cords out and threw the whole expensive computer system out the window. Ever since my brothers made sure not to have me do anything on the computer.

I'm a killer anyway, what I do is extract information and kill. I have no qualms about killing. I'm a wolf after all. I know how to stay alive because of it. I've gotten into some pretty sticky situations but always come out on top.

As my fist hovers next to Tyler's door, his low voice answers before I can even knock. "Come in." I open the door and watch as he stares intently at a computer screen.

"I just met Kat." That catches his attention because he completely ignores the five screens that he has opened. "I don't like her."

He rolls his eyes at me like I'm a dumbass. "Brother, you

hate everyone," he says, going back to what he was doing. I only grunt. "Did you find any info on why she has violet eyes?"

"Not yet, I'm still looking." He sighs like he's been trying to figure out this puzzle all day. "All the information is classified." He smiles wickedly. "But nothing can get past me. I'll figure it out soon."

"I'll talk to you later. I need to wash off and get some sleep." I haven't slept much in days, and I need to get some rest or I won't be able to function tomorrow. He gives me a small wave, not looking up from his computers. It's only a matter of time before he finds what we're looking for. Nothing stays hidden from Tyler very long.

Chapter 24

Kat

I t's Thursday, and the realization of today being the last full day I'll be married to Theo has my mind in overdrive. After tomorrow, I'll be a free woman. I'm torn between the relief of no longer being attached to someone who doesn't love me and finally being able to move on with my life outside my comfort zone.

Once I'm dressed, I leave my room to head to the kitchen. It's the kids' first day of school but I want to make sure I talk to Ava about what happened yesterday. I didn't want to interrupt her while she was making friends, but I have to make sure she's okay.

Az and I cross paths in the hallway. He's wearing a clean suit, and from what I can see, there's not a speck of blood. I can't smell any on him either. The red, slim-fit button-up and handkerchief compliments him, but it also makes him look sinister, and as much as I don't want to admit it, he's got the look down. His hair is held perfectly together with product to keep it looking sharp. He's definitely a drool-worthy example of a bad boy, and if I were smart, I'd stay far away from him.

Not that I have much of a choice in the matter since his living quarters are so close to mine.

"Sure, that's it. That's why it'd be hard to keep away from because of the close proximity." My wolf rolls her eyes at me.

When our eyes meet. He scowls and I smirk just to get on his nerves, but that cheeky smile turns downward quickly when I notice a pretty brunette trailing behind him down the hallway. I begin to clench my hands, hiding them behind my back so he won't notice. The last thing I want to do is give him ammunition to bother me further.

My wolf wants to leap out of this body and shred her to pieces. Damn she's ruthless. I keep a tight leash on her so she doesn't accidentally leap out.

She's short and dainty, I guess just like me. Us short people need to stick together so I try to give her the benefit of the doubt. My nose is up in the air, and... She smells like another breed. We walk past each other and my wolf is on edge waiting for me to get distracted so she can get out of her cage.

"Remember he and Ash are both assholes who made it perfectly clear they don't want us," I remind her.

Az turns around and faces his...friend, but keeps his eyes directed at me as he lowers his head getting closer to her. He whispers something in her ear too low for me to hear and she giggles. He opens the door to his room and lets her in, giving me a cold, dark smile before closing the door.

I just stand there for a moment, irritated by it. He obviously got really close to her to piss me off, but I'm glad to report that it did nothing for me.

"That sounds believable," she scoffs

I try and fail miserably to convince myself that all this stems from having to sign the papers tomorrow.

"Or it's because we have four hot men in this house and you want to do the nasty with all of them."

"Not true." I try to defend my human side, but we both know that's a lie. *"Okay, maybe only Tyler and Benji, but not the other two."*

"Yeah okay, keep telling yourself that." My wolf is leaking sarcasm now.

Before she does anything stupid, I walk down the hallway to Ava's room.

"Yeah, thanks. Just blame it on the wolf." Now she sounds irritated.

"Hey, Ava," I say when I get to her door. "Can I come in?" I knock lightly.

"Yeah come in, Mom." I walk in and she's already made this place her own. It's different from what she had at Theo's house. I never noticed how plain her room looked until seeing this one. It's bright pink with zebra accents. There's a beautiful window seat that overlooks the pool. I might have to borrow that idea because it looks comfy. Off to the side, she has two zebra print chairs.

I sit on her messy bed. "I want to talk to you." She nods her head and sits next to me. "About yesterday. I'm sorry about letting you go out there like that." When the words come out, I exhale deeply before I continue, but she stops me with a hand in the air.

"No, Mom, don't apologize. Ryder told me that the area is going to be marked before the shield ends so that it doesn't happen again." I still feel guilty that I didn't warn her before she left.

"I should have said something, Ava, and I am so sorry for that. I was so caught up in my head that I didn't register you couldn't see the barrier the same way that we can."

"Really Mom, it's okay," she insists. "And I need you to go so that I can finish getting ready for school."

"Did you want me to take you? I can get one of the guys and see if they'll drive us there."

"Cara is picking Ezra and me up," she says while getting up from the bed and going into her closet.

"Are you sure?" I make one last attempt.

"Yeah, I think we're good." These kids are growing up so fast, all they want is their independence.

"Okay well, I'm going to check up on Ezra," I say as I walk to the door. As soon as I'm out, she smiles and closes it immediately.

I walk to Ezra's room and knock. "Yeah," he shouts from the other side.

"It's Mom. Open up." I hear his heavy footsteps before the door swings.

"Hey, I want to check-in and see how you're doing since it's your first day of school. I can take you if you want."

"Nope, I'm good. Cara is picking us up."

"So I've heard. Well, If you need anything, just message me," I say with a smile.

"Thanks, Mom." He closes the door before I can get another word in.

As I make my way down the hall, I hear two sets of doors open and close. My kids are hauling their backpacks and practically sprinting out of the house. They seem eager to get the hell out of here.

"Bye, Mom," they say in unison as they storm past me.

"Love you guys. Hope you have a good day." A moment later, I hear them walking down the steps and closing the door.

With an angry sigh, I go back to my room, thinking about what Az and that brunette were doing alone. I wonder if he used those cuffs on her or what other secrets he has hidden in his locked closet. But I guess he's not the only one with a secrets.

I go to my nightstand and open the drawer. Now that I've slept and I'm not so tired from work last night, I can really look at what the sisters gave me.

I pull out the bronze and white trinket with intricate lines and press the cool metal into my palm. It's nothing like I've seen before. It looks like it was made ages ago and it probably was, but for the life of me, I can't figure out what the hell this is. There's a split that opens, but when I look inside the tiny hole, there is nothing. I shake it and then check the same spot again, but nothing has changed.

I'm not exactly sure how long I've been messing with this, but before I know it, it's noon and I go to the kitchen in search of some food.

There is a burger and some fries and a note from Lily.

I'm eating at the kitchen bar when my body stiffens and through my haze, I catch a whiff of Jasmine, Nutmeg, Ginger, Lavender, and leather.

Az.

I loosen my body and attempt to cover it up by acting like nothing's bothering me. "Where is Lily?" That deep voice hits all the way to my core and I have to suppress a moan.

I continue to sit there in silence eating my food, purposely ignoring him. Yes, I know it's petty, but he did tell me to stay out of his way and I'm helping him by pretending I'm not even here. This is definitely a childish move, but he irritates me and apparently brings out my inner brat. He annoys me more so than Ash does. No, that's not true, they both provoke me in different ways but are equally infuriating.

I didn't hear him come closer to me when he rests his

elbows on the bar standing dangerously close to me. If I even look in his direction, our lips will brush against one another.

My wolf is jumping up and down with excitement.

It's hard to ignore his closeness, but I manage anyway by stuffing my face with a few fries. In the back of my mind, I realize what I'm consuming but I do it anyway. "Ash told me you had a problem with eating your food, but it looks like you're being a good girl." *Good girl.* I clench my thighs together. Why did that word just affect me so much? It suddenly becomes harder to swallow my food. And why does Ash think I have a problem with eating? I've kept my figure by eating healthy and exercising regularly, nothing is wrong, everything is fine.

He moves one of his tattooed hands. I stare at them briefly, spotting black rose tattoos with black and red spider webs surrounding it. He's heavily tattooed, even more so than Ash.

I hold my breath when he picks one of my fries up and dips it in ketchup, bringing the food into his mouth. "You can't get your own plate?" I snap, surprised at how harshly it came out of my mouth. He only chuckles darkly and does it again. At this point, I think he's only doing it to get a rise out of me.

He's standing so close to me, I can't think straight. He's like a drug that I want more of. This intensity that I feel for all of them is starting to scare me. Maybe it's the wolf part? Or maybe I forgot what it feels like to want someone.

"It seems like you like to eat when I'm around." He's referring to the pie from last night. "Tell me, Kat," he purrs, and the way he says my name makes my skin blush. He gets even closer and whispers in my ear. "What else do you like to put in your mouth?" My eyes widen but I don't say anything.

He grabs my burger and takes a huge bite then sets it back on the plate. He smiles devilishly and leaves.

He's one of the strangest people I've ever met in my life. One moment he's cold and then he's hot.

Lilly walks back in. "Dear, why do you look so flushed? Where is Az?" She looks around the kitchen like he's going to appear from thin air. "I haven't seen him in two days," she complains.

Embarrassed, I clear my throat. "Oh, it's nothing," I say, throwing the rest of my food in the trash and putting my plate in the dishwasher. Avoiding her lingering gaze, I walk out of the kitchen as fast as I can.

CHAPTER 25

KAT

Today is the day that Theo brings me the divorce papers.

I'm so nervous about him coming here. I hope he doesn't try to start shit. "Everything will be fine, Mom," Ava says as she grabs a muffin before school.

I can't shake the unease in the pit of my stomach, but I try to push my worries aside and smile at her. "Yeah, everything is going to be alright." I agree, surprised out how convincing I sound when I feel anything but.

She looks so carefree; I don't want to burden her with my problems.

She checks her phone. "Oh, I gotta go. Cara will be here in a minute." Ezra comes to the kitchen looking grumpier than Ava. He probably stayed up playing video games.

"Hey, baby brother." He grunts as a response, picking up a muffin and slinking across the kitchen to grab his backpack.

"I'm not in the mood, Ava." He sounds groggy and annoyed. Definitely not a good combination.

"Bye, Mom! And remember, don't stress." I give them both a small wave.

When they came home from school yesterday, they were full of energy. They met so many supernaturals, and besides being the only humans there, they insisted the other kids were very welcoming.

I'm still surprised at how well they're taking all this supernatural stuff.

I grab my phone from the counter, checking to see if there are any messages from Theo.

There's only one.

Theo: Be there at 6pm

I don't bother messaging him back. I look at the muffin and decide to skip breakfast this morning. It has nothing to do with my eating habits and more to do with the way my stomach tightens at the thought of what's going to happen tonight.

Once I sign those papers, I'm a free woman. I haven't been free since I got married, well, more like since I met Theo.

"Hey there, Kitty Kat," Benji purrs in my ear as a trail of shivers goes down my core. How can his words get me so wound up?

"Hey, Benji." He looks smug like he knows exactly what he does to me.

"In a few hours you'll be divorced. How does it feel?" He drops his voice a notch making it sound seductive.

My breath picks up, and all of a sudden, all I can think about is having him on top of me, thrusting deep into me while I moan his—

Kat focus.

"I'm not sure. No, that's a lie. I'm scared down to my bones and..." I'm afraid to admit the truth, but I've been thinking about it for a while. "I think I'm a little relieved that it's finally happening." Maybe my nerves aren't from being scared but from feeling excited. I couldn't tell the difference until now.

I'm surprised my wolf side is calm, or maybe she's waiting to make an appearance tonight. Oh God, I hope not. She loves to react first and think later.

"You better not do anything to harm Theo." I tell her.

"What do you think I am? Stupid?" she growls, and I know she's not happy with me. *"I wouldn't risk Theo trying to take the kids away from us."*

"Well after your papers are signed, we can go on our date tonight. As much as I want to take you to a quiet dinner and have you all to myself, I want to watch you dance and let loose even more." He winks.

"Are we going to Crescent Lounge?" I already know the answer to that one. Since I can't leave their community, I know we have to stay here.

"Yep, but we'll still have fun, I promise."

I haven't danced in so long, I'm not even mad that we're going to the Crescent Lounge on my night off. It gives me something to look forward to after signing those papers.

"I have to get going, but I'll be here before Theo comes." I wasn't expecting him or any of the guys to be here, but I like the idea of having someone in my corner.

I bite my lip and smile. "Thanks. I appreciate the support."

"Anytime, Kitty Kat," he says, and I go back to day dreaming about having sex with Benji.

Once the cloud of lust passes, I go back to thinking about how in a few hours, I'm not going to be attached to anyone. Now I don't feel so guilty about lusting over the men that take up the space in this household.

Back in my room, someone knocks on my door. "Come in." I quickly put the metal object away along with Ash's tie and Benji's shirt. Before I can put Tyler's hoodie away, the door swings open.

Shit. Caught red handed.

Instead of getting angry, Tyler smiles widely. I find myself wanting to touch his sexy dimples, but I've got to focus on getting out of this situation.

I don't know if I should try to shove it back in the drawer and act normal or pull it out and hand it to him. I go with the former and shove it inside, turning to look at him with a smile on my face.

He chuckles. "I was looking for that hoodie, it's actually my favorite and the most comfortable one that I own."

"What hoodie?" I ask, playing dumb and looking around the room.

"It's okay, Kat, I'm not going to take it back." Good, because I wasn't going to give it back. "You can keep it," he says as he walks closer and sits on the edge of my bed. "Look, I came here to apologize. I should have told you that you couldn't leave against my brother's wishes. I shouldn't have kept you in the dark." He sighs deeply, rubbing his eyes. "I just really wanted you to like this place and everything would have been fine if I didn't step out. I didn't see anything out there." He laughs, but it sounds bitter.

I crawl on the bed and sit next to him, pulling his hands away. I stare into his chocolate brown eyes full of hopelessness. He actually thinks I'd hold a grudge over this. He's been really nice and welcoming to me, unlike the other two "I love this place and you're forgiven." His shoulders relax.

"Really?" he asks, sitting up a little straighter.

I nod my head, "Yes, really." To my surprise, he grabs my face and kisses me. I melt into his embrace. Being around him feels so natural and perfect.

He pushes me into the mattress and lays me back down, never leaving our embrace. Caging me in between his legs, he lets go of our lips and kisses my neck. I want so much more. I bury my hands beneath his shirt, and he lets me tug the material over his head without hesitation.

I run my fingernails down the length of his six-pack, which I've wanted to do since I saw him shirtless that first morning at breakfast. "I want you so bad, Tyler," I whisper in his ear.

"I want you too, Kat. You have no idea how much." And I know I won't like his next words. "But I think we should stop," he says with one last gentle kiss on my lips. "When you're finally free, we'll finish what we started." He pulls back from me and I whine.

"I don't care, Tyler. It's just a piece of paper, it doesn't change anything." But always the gentleman he smiles, standing up and taking off without another word. I grab his shirt from my bed and put it in my drawer along with his hoodie.

I don't know what it is with me and collecting their clothing, but I like having them around. Even the belongings of the two assholes that drive me over the edge.

After walking out of Kat's room, it takes every ounce of willpower to keep from turning around and going back to her.

"We should have stayed," my wolf says to me with longing.

Keeping my hand on my doorknob, I decide to go back and take her mind off things. I left in such a hurry, not even considering how stressed out she must be.

So I say *fuck it and* barge into her room without knocking.

She's lying on her bed and gasps when I stumble back into the room. She wasn't expecting it, and truthfully, neither was I. But I want to feel her soft skin and taste every inch of her until she forgets all about Theo's dumbass.

She gazes at me with hooded eyes, and the smell of her arousal puts me into a frenzy of want and need. "Kat..." Before I can say anything more, she runs toward me. I lift her up as she wraps her legs around my waist and begins kissing me frantically. She wants the distraction, and I'm happy to provide that.

I walk her back to the bed and lay her down gently, grabbing her shirt and pulling it off. I tug my sweats all the way down my legs and throw them onto her nightstand while she hurriedly unbuckles her pants. She gets them half down before I sit back on my knees and grab them, pulling them off her. She isn't wearing a bra and her breasts are on full display, just waiting for me to lick and suck them. I have to remind myself to enjoy this moment.

She sits up and slides her soft hand in between the waistband of my boxers and grabs my cock. She gasps slightly, running her fingers up and down the length of it. From the conversation I had with Benji, he told me she's not used to our length but she loved the feel of it when he was inside her.

She strokes me up and down slowly, taking her time. I hang my head low, reveling in the pleasure. Fuck, I want more. She swipes my pre cum with her thumb and brings it to her lips, sticking out her tongue and licking it clean. "Yum," she says playfully with a seductive smile, and my balls tighten.

I pull my boxers all the way down to give her more access. She bites her lip as she stares at my length. Fuck, this girl is going to make me cum just by staring at me.

As much as I want her to suck me off, I want to taste her first. She's been on my mind since I saw her distressed in the street and on the verge of turning. I wanted to chase her down and tell her that I'd keep her safe. My wolf was angry when we lost her.

I push her down gently and she looks at me with curious eyes. I lower myself in between her legs. As I lift my index finger up and my claw comes out, she lifts her brows in surprise and excitement. I bring one claw down and slide it across her panties, ripping it to shreds.

"Tyler!" she shouts. "Those are one of my favorite pairs

you bought me." She sucks her bottom lip between her teeth and it's all I can think about.

"I'll buy you more." I automatically reply, but my focus is on her bare cunt. Sure, I'll buy her new ones, but my attention is on my need to taste and devour her, not on clothing.

I look back at her violet eyes, so strange yet so beautiful. She wants this badly, she wants to forget about what's going to happen tonight, and I'm happy to help.

I lower my mouth and she moves her hips up, meeting me halfway. I smile at my needy, soon to be girlfriend, because that is what she'll be as soon as those papers are signed.

"Come on, Tyler. Stop messing with me." I chuckle, staring at her tiny bud just begging to be touched.

I lick in between her slit and she moans loudly. I want her every thought to be of me, to make her forget everything about Theo. I want to be in her head when she's signing those papers. I'm not as possessive as Ash or Az, but it's in my nature to be protective of the people I care about, and I care a whole lot about the woman lying under me.

"Do you know what you taste like?" I give her no room to answer. "Cherries. Sweet cherries." I don't ever want to go without tasting her again.

"She's mine," my wolf says, and I know that my eye color has changed.

I grab her pretty, soft breasts and groan at the weight. They're so perfect, just like she is.

I want more from her, and I know she wants more too. I thrust two fingers in her entrance and she tilts her head back, pushing her hips forward and giving me a better angle.

I suck on her clit while she fists the blankets, thrusting herself in my mouth. I want to fuck her so badly but decide to wait until she comes. I want to make sure she's fully wet before I try. I don't want to hurt her.

I nibble on her clit and roll my tongue in a rhythm she's enjoying. I can already hear her climax when she withers and screams my name. "Fuck that felt amazing, Tyler. No one has ever done that." I look at her completely puzzled.

"What do you mean? No one's licked this perfect pussy?"

"No, I've only been with one man and he didn't like that." My wolf growls. What the fuck, is this guy insane? "But even if he did, I doubt he'd be able to satisfy me as good as you have." She's got that right. I might be a nerd, but I do know how to pleasure a woman.

"So, what you're saying is that I should wake you up like this every morning?" She bites her lip with a huge grin. I know I'd be happy eating her for breakfast.

"Tyler, if you want to do that every day for the rest of my life I'd be the happiest woman in the world." Kat grins, taking my breath away. She's everything I never knew I wanted in a woman. All I want to do is make her happy.

I lean close to her mouth and kiss her gently while using my hand to guide my cock in between her legs.

She opens wider for me as I push deeper. "Fuck, Tyler, you're huge," she moans, pushing further. She's tighter than other women I've been with, and I think it's because she was born human.

Her walls constrict, and I stay still before thrusting because it feels like I'm going to combust. I haven't had this happen to me since I was a teen, and now I'm going to embarrass myself in front of my girl.

When I get ahold of myself, I start moving, feeling her walls twitch as I expand inside her. "Fuck this feels so good, Tyler. I don't think I'll ever get used to this." I chuckle, this is pure bliss.

I don't want to fuck her crazy, I want to make love to her

for our first time. This is something special between us. Benji and I both know this is something more than a few hookups.

She shutters against me as I trail kisses along her collarbone. I decide to bite her gently, nothing to mark her permanently, but when her husband comes, I want him to see it and know that she doesn't belong to him anymore.

I'm quite shocked by my thoughts. I'm not normally so possessive about a woman, but I want more with her.

I suck more and immediately feel her release. I pump harder into her, feeling my cock expand while she quivers around me and arches her back, bringing her breast closer. I bite down, her screams driving me on as I chase the wave of pleasure, letting her milk every drop from my cock.

Panting, I pull out slowly and lay down next to her, hauling her over to me and wrapping my arms around her. She leans back, accepting the comfort, and I hold her tighter.

I don't want to leave her by herself, but after a few more moments, I know I can't stay like this forever. "I have to go, Kat, and you have to try and get a bite to eat. I'll be back later." I give her a kiss on the cheek before I leave, grabbing my clothes and heading out of the room with a promise that I will be back to support her.

CHAPTER 27

KAT

After busying myself with nonsense all day long, the awaited moment is finally here. The moment where Theo and I sign the papers separating us from our marriage. This whole week has been leading up to this moment. It almost feels surreal.

All he wanted was for us to leave his home. He didn't care how I survived with the kids. The more I think about him and his actions, the more disgusted I am.

Faithful for sixteen years and this is what I get. Nothing but heartbreak. The only good thing that came out of that marriage were my kids.

A man walks right into the living room wearing a suit. He's clean shaven and wears his blond hair short. "This is Jack, he'll be your attorney." This guy is an attorney? My mouth hangs open, but I immediately compose myself. He looks way too young to be an attorney.

"They don't age like humans, remember?" My wolf rolls her eyes at me.

I honestly didn't think about finding an attorney and definitely should have, but I'm relieved to have someone on my side.

I stand up and shake his hand. "Nice to meet you, Jack." He lowers his head in a submissive manner, and I shift uncomfortably on my feet.

"It's very nice to meet you, Kat," he says in a gentle voice. Not what I expected from this guy. He entered the room like he was sure of himself, but inside the house he's timid.

"Are you flirting with her?" Benji's smooth tone interferes. He lays his head on my shoulder and grabs my waist. He's been getting super close lately but I don't mind it one bit.

"No…no" Jack stutters.

"Thank you for doing this," I interfere before he decides to run off because Benji is acting all Alpha like.

He lays his suitcase down. I have no idea what he has in there and I don't ask. Benji lets me go, and I walk back to the couch on the opposite side of the very young attorney.

It's five minutes before Theo should arrive, and my skin feels really itchy all over. "Calm down Kat or you're going to cut your skin and bleed all over the couch," Tyler says gently. My knee bounces up and down instead.

Az walks in looking bored out of his mind. Like he'd rather be anywhere but here, which makes me wonder what the hell he's even doing here. Maybe he wants to watch the waterworks, but I'm not giving anyone that. I've cried enough tears for Theo. I won't do it again.

The kids are out with their friends tonight so they don't have to witness what's about to happen.

I look at my phone again and it's six o'clock, and right on time, there's a knock on the door. I immediately jump up nervously. I heard their footsteps approaching but the knock on the door just made this whole situation real.

"You better get your ass to the front door or Benji will probably give Theo an ass beating. Although I wouldn't be opposed to watching that."

Shit, she's right. Benji has been playful, but underneath his relaxed appearance hides something more sinister. Something dark that wants to come out and play, and what better excuse than to unleash it on Theo. As much as I would love to see that, that's probably not the best plan.

I quickly run after Benji and Jack. Az and Tyler stay behind. Az sits in the corner of the living room with a leg over the armchair in a relaxed pose, twirling a knife in his fingers. He looks like my whole situation and existence is a bother to him, and I'm still wondering why he's here.

Tyler is on the opposite side of the fireplace wearing his glasses and typing away on a laptop. Two complete opposites. If I weren't so nervous, I'd laugh because it's crazy to think that these two opposites get along.

My heart beats so fast and I know that everyone in this room can hear it, but I don't care. I hold my breath when Benji finally opens the door and Theo comes in with angry eyes staring daggers at the man in front of him. Theo is assessing him like he does with everyone he talks to. He's a real dick like that. He likes to treat everyone based on their appearance.

The way Theo's eyes shift, I know he feels intimidated by Benji, and it's something that he doesn't like. He walks in further, taking in our surroundings while Benji narrows his eyes on my future ex.

I know exactly what Theo is thinking. He's wondering how the hell did I end up in this place and if I'm fucking the owner. I can't help the way my cheeks ignite in embarrass-ment, and that only pisses me off. I shouldn't care what he thinks about me anymore.

Theo assesses me and glares at the hickey Tyler left a few hours ago. His mood turning sour. "I see you've gained weight around your hips." My wolf growls but I keep my lips tightly shut. I watch as Benji, Az, and Tyler stiffen, and I know they're holding in the bomb they want to unleash.

There is another body following behind Theo, and though I'm surprised to see Dan, I shouldn't be. They're best friends after all. He's wearing a suit that really showcases his dark hair, fair skin, and caramel eyes.

When he spots me, his face turns into a huge grin. "I've missed seeing your lovely face." I watch as Theo narrows his eyes at him. But he doesn't give a care in the world that he might have made his best friend angry.

Dan has always been a flirt; it's in his nature just like Benji. He's always been respectful since I was with Theo, but now as he hugs me, his hands get a little lower, and I pull away quickly before they wander down to my ass. I hear growls in the background but I ignore them, focusing on the man in front of me.

"I've missed you too." Theo walks past us murmuring something I can't hear.

"I'm so sorry to hear about this, Kat," he whispers so low the other's won't be able to hear.

I pull away, grabbing his hands in both of mine. "Don't worry, it's better this way." I let go and start walking back to the living room with him next to me.

"How's Sarah?" He looks stunned, taken aback with the question. He's been a bachelor for so long, sleeping with lots of beautiful women. He usually never keeps longtime girlfriends, but he's taken Sarah out a few times already, so I think that relationship might be going somewhere.

"She...she's fine," he stutters. Okay, that was strange. Did he forget who she was? Or maybe he just broke up with her and doesn't want me asking questions.

I've personally met her and thought she'd make a good companion for Dan. The relationship looked promising.

Theo looks wary when he sees Az holding a dagger in his hands, giving him a cruel smile. Theo looks at me for an explanation but I only shrug. Secretly I hope that Theo is fucking scared and on the verge of pissing his pants. One can only hope though.

He makes sure to avoid Az's general vicinity, and I can help the small smile that's on my face. Little wins.

"Where are the kids?" he asks like he cares about them.

"They're hanging out with some friends." My heart beats faster for a moment, thinking that he'd fight me for custody, but he only shrugs.

"Are we ready to start?" Dan says in a chipper voice, and I'm so surprised that tone is coming out of his mouth at a time like this.

"Not yet," Jack says. "We need to wait for Ash."

As if he wanted to make a grand entrance, the man in question walks right in. "I'm sorry I'm late."

He walks into the living room, and I watch as both guys stiffen. There is a look of disgust on Dan's face, but he quickly changes it to the easy smile I'm used to. Maybe I just imagined it.

"I misplaced my tie somewhere in the office and spent quite some time looking for it." He says the last part with all his attention on me, and I want to hide under his scrutiny.

"Well, that's too bad. Maybe you should keep your

clothing in your room and not your office so it doesn't get lost." I wave it off and he only grunts as he takes a seat next to me. Without meaning to, my body leans closer to him, but I'm glad he doesn't say anything about it.

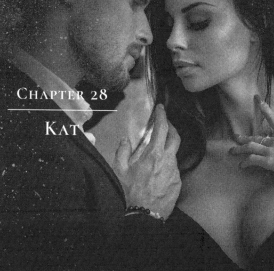

CHAPTER 28

KAT

I t's a long, gruesome process. I have no idea what's going on, but Theo's eye twitches when he hears any of the guys' voices. "She doesn't need anything from him. We'll take care of her and the kids." I see Theo's blood boiling, but what's more surprising is Dan's annoyed look.

Dan and Theo have been like brothers for a long time. I think he might feel like the guys are putting his friend down so he's getting defensive.

"Well, she can have the car if she wants it." Didn't he leave me without a car because he was trying to be a dick and that's how my whole mess started?

"I said no," Ash practically growls, and even Theo is surprised. "She doesn't need anything from you." His tone is as sharp as a knife.

Theo looks at me angrily, waiting for my response. I clear my throat "He's right. I have a job now. I can pay for it myself," I say proudly.

"What is it?" Theo demands. "Fucking all these guys?" He's trying to belittle me.

"Leave her alone." I'm surprised that it comes from Dan's

mouth. He quickly recovers and looks down at his papers. Theo's mouth hangs open and then turns into a scowl. I'm internally jumping up and down.

We go through back and forth banter until all of the papers are finally signed. "So, is there a waiting period, or are we completely done and the divorce is final?"

"I've got friends in high places, Kat." Theo says it like a threat. "All they need are these papers and we are done." Of course he has friends in high places. How could I have forgotten?

"Oh okay." I try not to show how much not being married is affecting me. But I'm a free woman now, and I can do whatever the hell I want.

It feels so good to finally have my life back. We all get up and Theo immediately walks out the door like he'd rather be anywhere else than here with us.

Dan, on the other hand, tries to reach out for a hug but immediately stops when Benji quickly pulls me away from him. Dan's features tighten in irritation, but he smiles when he looks at me.

"Bye, Dan. It was nice seeing you." I'm actually going to miss this guy. He's always been kind to me and the kids.

"You too, Kat. Please tell the kids that I miss them, and I can't wait to see them again. I'm their cool godfather."

I chuckle. "Of course I will." They both walk out the door and I feel lighter than I have felt in years.

Jack leaves shortly after. Az and Ash get up and leave without saying a word to me. I'm still reeling over the fact that they stayed and weren't rude to me. It seemed like they wanted to help me out.

"So what does it feel like to be a free woman?" Benji whispers seductively in my ear. He's still holding on to me, and I don't know if it's because I'm finally free, but I lay my head back on his chest, taking in the smell of pepper, amber wood, and citrus.

My body shivers as he trails kisses down my neck. When he turns me around, and I look straight into those beautiful green eyes, he lowers his mouth to mine. We are inches apart when he says, "I need you…" Ash growls out angrily. "Give me those reports that I asked you for." Benji sighs heavily.

I immediately step back from him. My face is hot, and I have no doubt it's as red as a ripe tomato.

Benji grins at me and looks over to Ash, narrowing his eyes.

Trying not to get in the middle of anything, I back away slowly. "I'm going to get ready for our date." I walk past Ash as he clenches his jaw. He's going to crack his teeth by how hard he's tightening it.

"I'll have the twins pick you up on their way, and I'll meet you there," he says before I'm completely out of sight.

"See you there." I wink. Wow, divorce is making me bold.

I get to my bedroom and close the door. I'm not sure what the hell that was about. I can't believe that mere minutes from getting a divorce I'm going to jump on the opportunity to be with Benji, and only hours before that, I was having sex with Tyler in my bed.

I need another girl's perspective. I grab my phone and message Jess.

> Me: Hey girl, are you busy?

> Jess: Not for you, and let me just say it's about damn time you message me back.

> Me: So the papers are finalized and I am a free woman.

> Jess: How do you feel about it?

> **Me:** I don't know…relieved, does that make me a bad person?

> **Jessica:** Absolutely not sweetie. It was about time you let go of that asshole in your life.

I bite my lip before saying this next part. I'm so scared about being judged, but I know Jessica will tell me straight up.

> **Me:** So Um…

> **Jess:** What's going on hun?

> **Me:** I had sex with two of the guys that live here before the divorce. Does that make me a bad person?

> **Jess:** Absolutely not. Theo made it perfectly clear he didn't want to be with you. Besides, life is too short. Let your freak flag fly.

Little does she know that I probably have a long life ahead of me now that I'm a wolf shifter.

> **Me:** Can you come over if I message you the address? We can celebrate my divorce and you'll know where I live.

I need to see my best friend and I don't care what they say, my bestie is coming to see me.

> **Jess:** Hell yeah I miss you and the kiddos.

> **Me:** I'll talk to you tomorrow. I'm partying tonight.

Jess: What!!! You're going out without me?
I'm jealous. You better get laid. Love ya Kat.

Me: Love you too Jess. Can't wait till
tomorrow.

I get up from the bed and decide to figure out what I'm going to wear tonight. I wish I had Jess here. I would have invited her tonight if it weren't for the supernaturals that are going to be there. I can hide it on a lunch date if we have it here, but a club full of non-humans would be difficult.

I don't try and think about what will happen when I tell Jess what I am. It's been a long and stressful day. Not just a day, it's been a week. I'll be happy to relieve some stress on the dance floor.

I curl my hair in loose waves, and when I'm done, I go through the closet and pick up a black, hollow-out mini dress with a knot on top and skin showing at the bottom. I try on the sleeveless dress and it hugs my curves perfectly. It's really flattering. Yep this is the one.

I put dark make up on my lids and add a bright red lipstick. I run my palms down the dress, enjoying the sleek feel of it before grabbing a pair of stilettos with a cute bow on the side.

I look at myself in the mirror and damn, I look hot. It's been a long time since I've felt this way, and it definitely didn't help my confidence knowing Theo was having sex with his assistant.

Benji said he'd meet me there. I walk out of my room and down the long hallway to meet up with Melissa and Sam. There's a car already waiting outside.

I open the door and get in the backseat. "Wow girl, you look sexy," Sam says from the driver's side.

"Divorce is looking good on you," Melissa agrees.

"Thank you," I say shyly, tucking a loose curl behind my ear and playing with the hem of my dress, feeling a little insecure. I need to snap out of this and have a good time.

"I can't wait to let loose tonight," Melissa says. "Liv is going to be there tonight and I've missed her so much," she says with a dreamy sigh.

"Girl, you look like a lovesick puppy right now," her sister laughs.

"Shut up," Melissa says through a light chuckle.

We get to the club, and instead of parking in the back like we normally do for our shift, we park in the front with the other patrons.

There are people outside drinking, talking, and having a good time. I'm amazed by all the different creatures waiting outside. Some have wings and horns, while others are a completely different color like blue and pink. I've never imagined so many different species existed in our world. My nerves are running rampant, and I wish I had Jess by my side.

We get out of the car and walk straight in. Benji is right, the music is poppin' and the colorful lights are blaring. It's darker than usual and so much more crowded tonight. I briefly think about all the tips I could be making but push the thought to the back of my mind. I should be having fun.

Melissa and Sam make their way through the thick crowd of dancing people. I go the opposite way to find the bar. I could really use a drink.

I'm squeezing myself through the crowd of people when I feel a hand on my waist and stiffen for a second before I recognize who it is.

Benji.

He grabs my waist and pulls me closer to him. My body leans into him quick to react to his touch. He runs his thumb through the front of the dress where my skin is showing. I inhale a sharp breath as he runs his nose down my neck.

"Kitty Kat," he says in a sultry voice. His words awaken other parts of me like Theo never could. "You look stunning in that dress." My skin burns with the need to touch him. "I'm jealous at how the men here stare at you with their greedy eyes. I need to show them you belong to me." He sounds a little possessive, but I actually like it. "Let's go dance."

I nod my head to agree. "But first, let's get a drink." My voice sounds husky.

"What do you want? I'll get them," Benji asks, his lips still hovering close to my ears. My eyes close, feeling the comfort of his voice.

"I want a lemon Martini." I open my eyes back up and search for a table, spotting one near the dance floor. "Oh and add some of that fairy liquor that makes us get drunk," I add. I'm planning to let loose tonight.

"I'll be right back." He reluctantly drags his hands away from my body, and I miss the heat of his closeness.

I make my way to the table before someone else takes it. I look around the place packed full of people. It's an adjustment to wrap my head around the idea that some people look like humans and others look like nothing I've ever seen before.

My neck and back stiffen with a tingling sensation. I look in the direction where I feel like someone is staring at me, but it's empty.

Huh, I could have sworn someone's eyes were on me.

Benji comes back, startling me. "Shit, sorry. I didn't mean to scare you." He sets our drinks down and I grab mine, some of the alcohol sloshing out on the table as I take a long ass sip. I've never had this drink before. I just saw it on the bar's menu and decided to try it. I'm so happy I finally did. This is so freaking good. "Woah, easy there, Kat. You don't want to get too drunk too fast." He gets up. "I'll be right back." He looks at the table. "It looks like you're going to be messy tonight," he chuckles as he leaves.

I'm watching the people on the dance floor when there's a brisk gust of air. I turn my head around but no one is in front of me.

Benji sits back down eyeing his drink with a slight frown. It looks to be rum and coke. He slowly brings it to his mouth and takes a sip, and as I bring my own glass to my lips, I realize it's already empty.

I frown at my empty drink and he chuckles. "I told you not to drink it so fast." And that's when the buzz hits me and I'm lightheaded and giddy.

I start swaying to the beat of the music. "You want to dance?" There's excitement laced in his voice.

I nod my head and that's all he needs. He grabs my hand and brings me to the dance floor.

We find a small space and squeeze ourselves in. He's behind me and I sway my hips side to side, enjoying this moment. It's been so long since I've danced that I forgot how much I missed this.

Throwing my hands in the air, I turn around to face him and look down, licking my lips when I notice the huge tent poking through his pants. "I can't help it, you look hot."

That's when the tingling comes back again. I turn back around facing the dance floor, trying to see if anyone is staring at me, but I don't find anyone.

Maybe it's all in my head. I'm judging myself for moving on so quickly.

I decide to move past those thoughts and let loose.

Benji's hands are on my hips, trailing down to my ass and

grabbing a handful. "What would you say, Kitty Kat, if I told you that I want to taste that sweet pussy of yours?" He lowers his hands to my entrance and there's an ache, a need that I've been wanting a very long time for. Theo and I stopped having sex a long time ago, and I've been neglecting myself. But not anymore.

Does telling him that sound too desperate? I try to keep it cool. "Yeah, let's get out of here." But my voice sounds needy. I grab his hand, pulling him from the dance floor and to the exit.

We walk outside holding hands. The need for Benji to touch me is unbearable. We make it to the next street where there are hardly any cars here and he pins me to the wall.

He claims my lips before lifting my dress up. "I've been waiting to taste you since I first laid eyes on you," Benji says as he lowers his hand and slides two fingers in between my folds, groaning when he feels how wet I am.

As he kneels in between my legs, my wolf howls in joy and both my human and wolf are in sync for once. He pulls off my black thong and throws it to the side.

There is something about being outside in the open where people can see us that makes this moment more intense. I can't believe I'm going to have this sexy as sin guy go down on me.

He stares at me like I've never been looked at before, and it tugs at my heart. There's compassion in his eyes that I've never seen in another man before, and I love it. He makes me feel beautiful, fierce, something I was missing for a very long time.

He gently trails kisses up my thighs and my whole body shivers wanting him to get closer to me. I roll my head back onto the wall breathing heavily. "I want you to watch me, Kat," he snaps and I look down to where he's kneeling.

"Remember, Kitty Kat. I'm an Alpha and I kneel for no one."
His tone is low and dangerous which only makes me wetter.

I brace myself and open wider for him. I can't believe I'm
exposing myself to him, giving him more access. He gives
me a saucy grin in return, hovering over my cunt. It feels like
I'm standing here forever until I feel his tongue running
across my slit. He's alerted my whole body with one lick, and
I don't think I can ever go back to not having this.

He tastes and sucks, and the whole time my body builds
in anticipation. "Fuck, Benji. This feels so good," I cry out.

As if what I tell him is motivation, he works harder to try
and get me to cum. "I'm almost there." My legs begin to
shake. The last thing I remember is screaming out his name
when my body shatters. I've never in my life had an orgasm
this strong.

I'm panting so hard like I've just ran a marathon when a
recognizable voice booms through the dark night, startling me
from my high. "I didn't take you for being a slut."

CHAPTER 29

KAT

"I didn't take you for being a slut." Benji quickly composes himself and turns his back on me in a protective stance.

There is nothing of that lightheartedness I saw from Benji earlier. This man is pure animal, ready to defend and attack.

I pull my dress down immediately trying to compose myself and stare at the man in shock. "I...thought you left." I stutter.

"Well, you see Kat, I can't leave." I scrunch my brows in confusion. I'm not sure what he means. Did he forget some papers? And even if he did, why does he look so angry?

"Why are you still here?" Benji growls. "You were supposed to be escorted out."

Dan chuckles darkly, and it's something that I've never heard from him before. My skin prickles. This doesn't sound like the Dan I know at all.

"You see, Kat, when Theo said he was going to leave you, I thought finally you could be mine. I've always admired you from afar." I swallow through a thick lump in my throat thinking back on all those times he used to flirt with me. "I knew if I intervened, you still wouldn't leave Theo. So I bided my time patiently, knowing that it was only a matter of time before he fucked up."

"She's not going anywhere with you." Benji's shoulders are tense like he's ready to leap out and attack at a moment's notice.

"That's where you're wrong, wolf." And my mouth hangs open. He knows what they are. "You see, she's mine...I bit her." His eye color changes and I nearly fall to the floor, his words bouncing around my head, surely to haunt me for the rest of my life. How could he? What made him think that he could scare me in an alley and bite me to turn me into a wolf?

"Enough talking," Benji says, ready to leap out when a tranquilizer dart touches his neck. I scream but my man gets back up. *My man?* It didn't affect him at all. He takes it off his neck and throws it to the side. "Now you fucked up." That's when another one goes in his neck and he crouches down on all fours, his eyes changing colors.

It looks like he's trying to change but can't. He takes that one off. His eyes are looking droopy. Shit. This is not good.

I look around to see who's shooting Benji, but the only other person I see is Dan. "What are you doing?" I stare at him, my blood boiling. "Please stop. You're hurting him." I plead, but he shows no remorse.

"I should kill him but that would start a war that I have no interest in fighting. I just came here for what's mine."

"No. You're not fucking taking her." Benji manages to get up, but it looks like he's struggling to talk. His face is turning red and I'm getting worried for the sweet guy, who just moments ago gave me the best orgasm I've ever had.

"I'm not going anywhere with you," I say in a shaky

voice, shocked that Dan has been waiting for the moment to take me from Theo all along. "What will Theo think when he finds out?" I ask, playing the best friend card.

He scoffs. "I don't give a flying fuck about him." At my shocked expression, he continues. "The only reason I tolerated him was because I got the chance to be around you." My heart beats rapidly. "Oh, Kitty Kat," I narrow my eyes at him for using my nickname. "What? Only Benji can call you that?" he pouts. "I should have that privilege too."

"Don't call me that." I snap back.

He ignores me. "I hear your heartbeat, there is no reason for you to be scared of me." My shoulders tense. "So you see, Kat, it was never about him. This was always about you." He gets closer, and I try to take a step back, but I'm against the wall already.

"Get away from her." Benji's voice sounds weaker, but he's still trying to put up a fight. He stands again, and that's when another one hits him and he finally goes down. He tries to keep his eyes open, but he's fighting a losing battle.

I run to him and fall to my knees, tears streaming down my face as his eyes flutter shut. I take the dart from his neck and toss it on the ground.

"We can do this the easy way or the hard way. I prefer if you cooperate, but either way, you'll be mine."

"I'm not coming with you," I say in my fiercest tone, even though I've never felt weaker.

He shrugs and his eyes blaze. "I guess we'll do it the hard way then." The sound of an engine gets closer. I look to my right, still kneeling on the ground. A black SUV limo comes into view, and someone opens the door for me to get in, and that's when I spot my kids lying down as if they're sleeping.

They've been tranquilized too.

No, no, no. This can't be happening. "As I said, we can do it the easy way or the hard way." As soon as he finishes those last words there's a sharp pain in my neck.

The world spins around before everything goes black.

CHAPTER 30

KAT

I wake up, looking around my surroundings. This feels oddly familiar. There's light coming through the windows, which means it's the next day. I try to sit up as best as I can, moving my hands to help me, but they're cuffed to the bed. I try not to panic.

The memories from yesterday hit me like a freight train. "Good morning." There's a smooth voice coming from the entrance of the room. I've heard it so many times over the years. Never once have I thought he had ill intentions toward me or my family.

A thought hits me, something that I should have noticed ages ago. Dan never aged. I guess I always thought he was blessed with genes kind of like how Pharrell the singer never seems to get older.

He walks from the doorway and sits on the edge of the bed. He has a new scar that I didn't notice earlier that starts just above the eyebrow and ends slightly below the eye.

He watches me as if he knows what I'm staring at. "It's the knife you stuck in my eye right before you scratched up my face pretty good." I flinch away from the heat of his breath on my face as he leans closer. "I covered it up yesterday so no one would see it."

I almost feel bad about fucking up his face until I remember the reason I'm here. "I can't believe you kidnapped us," I say as I try to bring my knees up to my chest but remember I'm wearing a tight dress with no underwear. I try not to cringe at the thought of leaving my underwear out in the open like that, but there are more pressing matters at hand.

He watches my legs with so much need in his gaze, but I want nothing from him. I straighten my legs on the bed and hide underneath the blankets. It provides a sense of security, so I don't feel completely exposed.

I can't help but wonder if maybe it would have been different between us if he told me about Theo cheating. Or if he didn't fucking bite me. I'm still bitter about it knowing I could have died.

"I thought you had a relationship with Sarah." His eye slightly twitches in annoyance and I wonder if Sarah was just for show. He brought her to meet me a couple of times, and he never brings the same girl twice, so I thought she meant something to him. Sarah thought they were building a relationship, at least from what she'd informed me.

"You'll love this pack," he says roughly, switching the conversation like I hadn't asked about one of the girls he brought to Theo's house.

He sits closer to me and tries to touch my face, but I flinch away, and he puts his hand down like he doesn't notice. His nostrils flare and he bares his teeth when he zones in on the hickey Tyler left behind. Oh, Tyler, my sweet man. He must be panicking right now trying to figure out where the hell I am. "You're very special, Kat. I just hate that Theo got to you first." I'm surprised he says his name with so much venom. "He didn't deserve you."

I call on my wolf to see what she thinks about all this, but she's as confused as I am. She sees all the memories of Dan and never once suspected him of having ulterior motives.

"But Theo," I say as I still can't wrap my head around this. "You always hung out with each other. He is..." I scrunch up my face since that doesn't sound completely right anymore, "or I guess was your best friend."

"He means nothing. He was a means to an end and that was for me to get to you." This time he manages to touch my face even when I try to move from his grip.

"Where are my kids?" I ask. I know he wouldn't hurt them, he is their godfather after all. Damn, he really fooled us all.

"They're eating breakfast in their room. Why don't you take a shower and I'll have someone bring some breakfast up for you." Shit, this means I'm not on the bottom level. It might prove difficult when I try to escape. He finally lets go of my face and I can breathe easier. "There are clothes for you in the drawer." He rolls his eyes at my dumbfounded look. "I know your size, Kat. I know everything about you." I gulp loudly not liking the sound of that.

"I'm not yours, Dan," I say softly, looking down at the blankets.

"You belong to me, Kat. I bit you. Well, not just mine, but the other Alpha's too." I look up into his eyes and swallow through a thick lump in my throat. I never thought there would be others, but I should have guessed. Benji told me there's four shifters to one female. "You'll meet them later tonight. We're having a celebration in your honor," he says excitedly as I suppress the urge to puke. "We've all been waiting patiently for our prize." *Prize?* What the fuck, I'm no trophy.

"Why did you bite me? I could have died." I cry, tears welling up in my eyes.

"No, Kat, you're special." He tucks my hair behind my ear and I slightly flinch. It feels more intimate than it should. "I knew you'd survive."

"Do you have a phone I can borrow?" His body stiffens and I immediately continue. "So I can call Jess, we were supposed to meet." He looks at me for a moment. Probably debating whether or not to hand it over.

He pulls it from his pocket and I immediately reach for it but am quickly reminded that I'm handcuffed. "Those guys told you about the curse right?" But before I can ask him to clarify, he continues. "You can message her but I need to see what you write before you send it." I nod my head and grab the phone.

I'm grateful I memorized her number.

> Me: Hey it's Kat. I'm using Dan's phone since I lost mine. I have to cancel our plans for today, something has come up and I won't be able to make it. I'll message you again when I get my phone so we can plan something soon.

I hand the phone back for him to read, and once he's satisfied, he presses send.

I have to come up with a plan to get the hell out of here. I wonder how he was able to get me out with that spell they put on the border so I couldn't leave?

"I'm going to go shower," I tell him sweetly trying to get him not to suspect that I want to be by myself to plan my escape. I seem to think better in the shower.

He pulls out a key and unlocks the cuffs. "I'll be back to

see if you need anything." I put on the fakest smile I've ever had. He buys it because he grins right back.

When he leaves the room, I jump straight to the shower. It's not as impressive as the one at home. *Home?* It's what it means to me now.

"What do you think, wolf? How the hell do we manage to get out of here?"

"During the party tonight. It's our best chance."

She's right, it has to happen tonight. I can't stay here. I develop the scheme in the shower and get excited to put the plan in motion.

CHAPTER 31

BENJI

I wake up in bed feeling frantic, realizing that I'm in my room. The guys probably picked me up when they didn't see me with Kat. They should know by now that she's gone. I wonder if anyone has told the kids yet. I should be the one to tell them that I lost their mom. I grab my hair tightly wanting to rip it out with so much anguish.

"This is going to suck," my wolf says sadly.

Looking at the clock, I realize that the tranquilizers had me sleeping all night and most of the morning. It's almost noon. This is not good at all.

The guys are probably impatiently waiting for me, wondering what went down last night. I get dressed quickly and head downstairs.

"What happened? We tried to wake your ass up, but you were dead to the world." Ash wastes no time as I walk into the office. He's pacing around like a madman in distress. Although he acts like he doesn't care for Kat, she's starting to grow on him. He feels like he doesn't deserve love, but in reality, he's one of the people that should have it.

Az stands as still as a statue in a dark corner, ready to strike at a moment's notice.

"I don't fucking know," I say feeling guilty. I could have taken Dan of course, but I wasn't expecting the tranquilizers. "Kat and I were having our fun two blocks down from the Crescent Lounge when Dan showed up pissed and ready to take Kat away. I was prepared for a fight, ready to protect our girl, but I got hit with a fucking tranquilizer," I say, touching the spot on my neck where the first one hit. Nothing is there anymore because we heal fast, but this dose was made for shifters. That's why it put me to sleep. "He had help. I don't know how many, but he wasn't working alone." I feel as though I'm missing crucial information, but my head is pounding.

If Ash grips the back of the chair any harder, he'll break it. He's barely controlling his rage, and when he lets out that beast, all hell will break loose.

"The kids are gone too," Tyler says as he walks into the office.

Both my wolf and I feel like we've failed. *"We need to find them."* My wolf begins pacing back and forth the same way Ash is doing.

"I don't have anything yet. But I'm going through the face recognition software waiting for information to pop up."

I tug on my lip thinking about what we're missing. It's there at the tip of my tongue. Oh shit. "Dan is Dante, as in the person who bit her." My brothers look stunned.

"How was he able to go undetected when he came to our home and signed the papers? We're Alphas, we should have been able to smell him as our own kind or we should have known that he wasn't human." Ash's eyes are changing color, and I think he's losing control and might shift.

I grab the sides of my head. I can feel a headache starting to form behind my eyes. This is a mess.

"How was she able to escape the borders? It shouldn't have let her leave?" Tyler touches the bridge of his nose trying to put the pieces together.

"About that," Az says, still hiding in a corner. I almost forgot he was there. "When we went near Kat's house on Monday looking for our target, I noticed a strange scent. He might be working with someone powerful."

"Shit," I say. "This just made our situation more complicated."

"This is not looking good, guys," Tyler whines, leaning against the door.

"Do we have any guesses on what pack Dante might belong to?" I couldn't get a read on him when he was here, which means he is working with someone strong. "Maybe he works for the council and was told to make her into a wolf." It sounds strange, and it's not something they'd usually do.

"Yeah, but for what purpose?" Tyler asks. It's a possibility but not a likely one. They were firm about their stance on creating any more wolves.

Everyone shakes their head, if the council promised wolves torture and then death, they wouldn't sway so easily. "I'll do another search with only shifters. It should shorten the time if there is a database on him. I'll also look up his current address based on his human profile since we know it's Dante. I'll ask Jack what his last name is and I'll pull up the search." Tyler walks out of the room.

"Az, go check who was on guard duty and figure out why they didn't escort all the guests out." Ash says in a barely controlled voice. "And then kill them." Az walks out with a carefree step, but I know my brother, and he can't wait to figure out who fucked this up and make them bleed.

"Benji, ready the bombs. As soon as we have an address from Tyler, I'll get the enforcers to check the place out. We're getting her and the kids today." This is my favorite part, blowing shit up.

"I'm going to contact Ryder, Bryson, Zay, and Cash. They've been blowing up my phone nonstop." I haven't checked mine, but I'm sure they've been trying to get a hold of me.

"Tell them that I just woke up and haven't seen my phone yet." I don't want them to think I'm purposely ignoring them. He nods and I leave the office.

"We're coming for you, Kitty Kat," my wolf howls.

CHAPTER 32

KAT

After my shower, I find a pair of jeans and a tank top with some racy pink lingerie on the bed. I check the drawers but they're all empty. Ugh... I really don't want to wear this, but it looks like I have no other option. There are no other clothes. I quickly get dressed and find breakfast on the table.

It's an omelet and I devour it quickly. I get up and try to twist the knob on the door but it's locked. Figures.

I need to get to my kids and make sure they're fine. I pound on the door. "Hey, let me out." I keep doing it a few more times until I realize it's no use. No one is going to come.

I look out one of the two windows, noticing there are security bars, but I can still manage to see how high up I am. I'm about three stories high. I can make the jump in my wolf form. I grab the bars and smoke comes out. I let out a high-pitched scream at the pain in my hands, looking down at the red welts that bloom across my shaking palms.

What the hell?

Dan slams the door open with an older lady trailing behind him. "Were you trying to escape?" His tone is accusatory with an underlying hurt crossing his features, which pisses me off, but I rein in the anger.

"Come sit down," the lady says. I walk back to the bed and sit. "Show me your hands." I unclench my fists and face them palms up. She grabs them both to inspect them and pulls an ointment from her bag. As she lathers it all over my skin, there's an instant cooling sensation and relief filters through me.

"Thank you," I tell the lady with kindness. I'm not going to be rude to her, I have no reason to be. She's not the one that kidnapped me.

When the lady leaves, I turn back to Dan with a glare. "I was trying to figure out how to get to my kids. I need to make sure they're fine." I cross my arms trying to be careful not to get the ointment on my clothes.

He studies me for a moment, trying to decipher if I'm lying. "Okay, I'll bring them here. You guys can hang out before the party starts."

I nod my head and he goes to walk back out. "I'm not the bad guy, Kat."

I know I shouldn't, and it's best to keep my mouth shut, but my mouth opens before I can think this through. "Really? Where the fuck were you when Theo was treating me like shit?" I accuse.

"You wouldn't have believed me," he retorts, and I roll my eyes.

"You could have taken pictures and done something more than stand on the sidelines watching him hurt me." He could have warned me long ago and spared me so much heartache, but of course, that wouldn't have been part of his plan.

"You have no idea how hard it was for me not to kill him

for all the shit he put you through, but if I ever laid a hand on him you wouldn't have believed me." He pleads for me to understand, but I don't want to hear it. He should have done something. All he cared about was the end goal, for him to have me and not view him as the bad guy. But that's where he's wrong. I see him as the villain because he could have prevented so much heartache for me.

I turn my head away from him, making it clear that I don't want to have this conversation anymore. I hear the door close and my shoulders relax. I want to cry from all the emotions I've been through over the last week but hold it together not wanting my kids to see me break down.

A few moments later, the door opens and my kids walk in. They look bewildered. "Mom," they both say at the same time, rushing to give me hugs.

The door closes and we are left alone. "Do you know why Uncle Dan is keeping us here?" Ezra asks, scrunching his face.

"One moment I was hanging out with my friends, and the next, I see them all dropping like flies, then everything went black and we ended up here. I was freaking out until I saw Uncle Dan." Little does she know that he's not as he seems.

I think about what to tell them and settle for the truth. If I were in their situation, I wouldn't want anyone lying to me. "So the bottom line is that your uncle is not the person we thought he was. He kidnapped us all, and I'm pretty sure he wants us to stay with his pack."

"What!" Ava yells. "No, I can't stay here, I want to go back." She shakes her head, only a moment away from having a nervous breakdown. I'm starting to wonder if this is about her new friends or a certain blue-eyed boy we left behind.

"Yeah, I don't want to stay here either," Ezra agrees.

"And we're not," I say quietly, so they are the only ones that hear me. I don't know if we're being watched but better safe than sorry. They nod their heads in unison. "One more thing," I say in my normal voice. "Dan is the one that bit me and why I became a wolf."

"What the fuck?" Ava shouts. Ezra's mouth is wide open in shock.

"Language mija," I say sternly. "I am just as shocked as you two."

"I wonder what Dad would think," Ezra voices.

"He doesn't care. You know that Ezra." And my heart hurts for the sad look that crosses their faces. I sigh tirelessly, I'm not sure how to answer that one. "I don't know," I finally say.

We spend the rest of the day watching movies. There is not much that we can do while we're stuck in this room. None of us have cell phones.

Someone brings us food but that's about it. Dan doesn't show up at all.

Later in the evening, there's a knock on the door and someone walks in holding clothes in their arms.

"It's time to get ready," the lady says. "The kids will go to their room and get ready." My kids look back at me with wide eyes.

I get up from the bed and my shirt rides up a little. My daughter gasps loudly. "Mom, when did you get that tattoo?" I look down to the wolf, forgetting for a second that it was there.

"Oh, it showed up when I became a wolf."

"Looks badass, Mom," Ezra comments as he looks at my inked skin.

"Language hijo." Once they've stared long enough, I

usher them to the door. "Go," I tell them. "Tonight will be fine." I wink at them and they relax a bit.

"Bye, Mom," Ezra says sadly and my heart hurts for my kids. I watch as two strangers wait for them outside.

"Protect."

Yes, I need to get them out of here. The lady lays the dress on the bed and I can already tell Dan picked this out. It has his sense of style written all over it. I remember seeing dresses like this when he'd be with other women. Now I know he picked out their outfits too.

"Please sit." I walk over to the dresser and fall into the chair. She styles my hair in loose curls that sit just above my butt. Another woman walks in with a luggage full of makeup, and I sit quietly while they primp and polish me.

It's really unlike me to be silent and not start off a conversation. That's how I know Dan really pissed me off. Normally, I would try to be friendly and find something to talk about, but I have no enthusiasm to put on a fake smile.

When they're done, I can't help but admire how good these two are. I look hot as hell. I just wish my men were here to see this. I know they aren't really mine.

I haven't gotten a chance to really think about how Benji's doing. I hope he's okay. I really miss him and Tyler. The other two are assholes. My little heart flutters at the thought of them anyway.

I strip down quickly and grab the scarlet dress, slipping the soft material over my head and letting it fall across my hips. It's long with a trail of sequences that opens in a V down to my belly. There is a slit on both sides of my legs. I'm not wearing a bra or underwear since I took them off earlier. I feel exposed. I put on the matching red heels that are adorned with sequence.

Fuck! I can't say I hate the dress, I just hate the person who bought it for me. I watch the doorknob turn and I know it's going to be Dan. So far, he's been the only one who doesn't knock before barging in.

He looks at me, his face flushed. "Kat, you look gorgeous in that dress." Normally, I would comment on how handsome he looks, and though I can certainly still see the appeal he has to other women, all I see now is my hatred. He's wearing a suit that hugs his hard-earned muscles in a way that would drive most girls wild. He works out as much as Theo, and I've seen him plenty of times without a shirt on, but it does nothing for me now that I know what kind of man he really is.

I stay silent and he comes close to me, grabbing my face forcefully. Already knowing what he wants, I turn my head away from him and his lips land on my cheek instead of my mouth.

"Come on," he says, grabbing my hand, but I pull away quickly and fold my arms together. "You're going to have to get used to your new normal."

He walks and I follow his lead. As soon as I leave the bedroom, I know we're in Dan's house. I've been here a handful of times but never to any specific room. We go down three flights of stairs. "Where are Ava and Ezra?" I ask, thinking we were going to meet them before we all go outside.

"Oh, they're hanging out with their friends. I bet they've been missed." I stop breathing. No, no, no, how are we supposed to get away? We need to escape today. "Is something wrong?"

I recover quickly. "I'd like to know this information before you make a decision like that."

"I wouldn't let them go anywhere that wasn't safe for them. I am their godfather after all, Kat," he snaps as if I hurt his feelings by not trusting him with my kids.

"Well, as their mom, I'd like to know where they are at all times, Dan."

"Fine," he grumbles.

He leads me out of the backdoor and down a long paved path I'd never seen before. There are fairy lights strung over a large alcove, and the music echoes through the trees surrounding his property. Unease grows in the pit of my stomach when I see how large the crowd is.

Theo puts a hand on my exposed back, reminding me that I'm almost naked in a large gathering of dangerous-looking strangers. The chattering completely stops as we come into sight. "Silver Dawn Pack. This is Kat. Kat, this is some of the wolves in our pack."

I look around at the people waiting in silence, expecting me to say something. I clear my throat. "Hi everyone." They smile in approval and go back to whatever it is they were doing. All of them talk among themselves, and I can't help but feel like I'm being judged. I hate it, it's like living in Theo's world all over again.

I try to school my face to remain calm, although my nerves are getting the best of me. We walk to a long table at the head of the party and I sit reluctantly next to Dan.

"The rest of the pack members will be here soon." My knee bounces up and down with nerves, thinking about how I'm going to get out of here and get to my kids so that we can escape.

Dan eyes my bouncing legs with soft compassion, mistaking my nerves for something else. "Kat, the other guys will love you just like I do."

There's a version of me that would have loved to hear those words from any man after what I went through with Theo, but I'm not that broken woman anymore. My pack mended me in ways I never knew I needed, and staring into Dan's eyes now, all I want to do is punch him in the face for what he's done.

Three tall, bulky guys approach us, and I can tell these guys are the other Alpha's. They are the complete opposite of Dan with tattoos adorning their shaved heads. I swallow through a thick lump in my throat and glare at them.

Dan stands up and tries to hold my hand, but I pull away at the last minute. Everyone has gotten quiet, it's like they're waiting to see our interaction.

"Kat, I would like you to meet Liam, Samuel, and Christian." He smooths his suit as he looks over the other men in front of us.

"Keep their gaze," my wolf tells me.

I do what she says because she knows more about this world than I do. They stand across the table in front of me and Dan. Dan grabs my arm instead, pulling me up with him.

"Dante." My head immediately snaps to the man sitting next to me. What the fuck? Did I hear that right?

I always thought his name was Daniel and we called him Dan for short. Shit, I should have known. "You managed to get her back," Samuel says, not looking at me once. "How is she liking her stay?"

Umm… does this man not see me standing right in front of him.

"She's getting acquainted," he chuckles.

"I'm glad," Chris says, ignoring me too. What is it with these guys and acting like I'm not right in front of them?

"She's gorgeous." The one on the left eyes me in a way that sends chills creeping up my spine. It's nothing like the chills I get from Az or even Ash. This one gives me the creeps. His smile only widens when he notices my discomfort. I have to keep my eye on that one.

He lowers his gaze down to my breasts, and I wish I had something to cover my body. He's giving me psycho vibes.

I sit back down since they're talking about me like I'm not even here. The only normal one is Dan...Dante. Fuck, that's going to take some getting used to.

When the food comes out, my stomach is doing somersaults. I have no appetite. As if sensing my discomfort and assuming it was the presence of food causing it, Dan shakes his head sadly. "Babe, I know Theo was a dick about what you ate, but I won't ever be." His words are gentle but the harsh way he called me a slut when he found me in the alley still plays in my mind on repeat.

All I want to do is grab the plate and throw it in Dan's face. I smile and grab a fork to keep my ruse, bringing some mashed potatoes up to my mouth. He smiles widely and goes back to eating like he has no clue that I'm trying to escape. Just like I want it to be.

I look around at the eyes trained on me from every direction. Escaping will be much harder than I'd expected.

"Can we stop by and check on the kids after we eat?" I whisper to Dan. I can't leave without my kids.

He has a mouthful of food but nods his head.

I have to try and relax or else they'll hear my heart pounding erratically and notice that something is wrong. Their suspicion is the last thing I need right now.

Samuel stands up, smiling at everyone. "I want to make a toast..." and that's all he gets to say before all hell breaks loose.

Screams are all around us, and all I can think about is being grateful that my kids aren't here. Dan grabs me, and I try to pull my hand away from him. "I'm trying to help you," he growls. I let him pull me underneath the table. He's in mid shift, his hands and mouth are no longer human, but even seeing him now, I still can't wrap my head around him being a wolf, let alone the person who turned me into one.

There are bombs going off, and I fear for my life as the booms get closer. I need to get out of here and get to my children.

I reach out and grab a handful of dark fur before he's able to race off into the night. "Dan, the kids." He watches the tears pool in my eyes and nods his head in understanding. I can see his hesitation; he's worried I'll try to escape in the chaos, but he knows I would never leave without my kids.

He slides out from under the table, leaving his expensive suit in shreds on the ground in front of me. People are screaming, shifters growling, and limbs flying everywhere. A piece of an arm falls right in front of the table I'm using for cover, and I try my hardest not to gag.

I watch the scene unfolding and there is so much carnage. Wolves are savages. I make sure that Dan is distracted before I try to escape, but another bomb goes off and pieces of a shifter rain down over my face. I duck back beneath the table and try not to panic, but I'm terrified to go out there. I don't want to get blown to pieces before I find my kids and get them home safely. My heart thumps wildly. It's now or never. I brace myself and start running.

I can feel the wind on my face and the air is filled with the smell of copper. I almost make it out of the property when a voice stops me in my tracks. "Where do you think you're going, Kat?" Chills run through my body at his venomous voice. I decide to pay him no attention and continue to run, but he grabs the back of my neck and holds me in place.

"You're not thinking of escaping are you?" Liam whispers in my ear.

"I'm trying to get to my kids to make sure they're fine." There's a bead of sweat that trails down my neck, and Liam focuses on it like he wants to lick it. God I hope he doesn't. I don't want that tongue anywhere near me.

"You should wait for Dante." My eyes widen and he laughs darkly at my shocked expression. "I was within hearing distance to make sure you didn't explode."

My mind is running wildly trying to figure out how I'm going to get out of this situation. He has a tight grip on my neck to the point where his claws are digging deep into my skin.

While I'm having an internal debate, I hear a loud growl from my right side. There's a wolf jumping straight at us. I squint my lids shut preparing for the impact. After a few seconds when nothing happens, I open my eyes and am staring at one of the men I thought I would never see again.

"What the fuck are you doing, Liam?" I can't say I've ever been as happy hearing his voice as I am today. His voice holds so much authority. Liam's grip on my neck eases and I turn my head to look at him, noticing traces of fear in his gaze.

Hmm…interesting. So Liam is afraid of Ash. "This is my territory and you and your pack should have called if all four of you were coming. Not only that, but you guys have been keeping the fact that Dante is a new Alpha with your pack and has been here for a while without my pack's approval." His tone is so menacing that even I stand up straighter.

Liam looks confident but his tone says otherwise. "We apologize for intruding and—"

"If you would have told us, we could have saved you all the slaughter," Ash says angrily, and it dawns on me that they are the ones that planted those bombs that could have easily killed me. My face gives away my emotions as always. "Relax Katarina, we knew exactly where you were at all times. We wouldn't have blown you up." Yeah right. That would have been an easy way for him to get rid of me.

We turn to look at the massacre and nearly all the shifters that I had seen earlier are all dead on the floor. I swallow hard. Who are these people I've been staying with?

"Definitely assassins," my wolf says.

"Yup," I agree with her.

"This could have all been prevented," Ash says in a derogatory tone which has Liam growling softly.

"We'll just take her with us and you'll never have to see us again." Ash laughs like Liam just told him the funniest joke.

"Oh Liam, she's not going anywhere with you."

"Dante bit her, she's ours." I don't think I'll ever forgive him for that.

"Yeah, he bit her in our territory, which means we decide the rules, and we have decided to keep her." Ash stands up to his full height and it's terrifying.

Dante finally shows up with anger in his eyes. "No, I'm taking Kat. She's mi...ours." He corrects his slip up, and I'm wondering if he would even share me with the rest of the Alpha pack members. They're all really different from Dan.

"If you don't want to be blown up into little pieces like we just did your crew, then you will leave our dearest Kitty Kat to us," Benji says from behind me.

I turn around to look at him, and the playful flirty man is gone, replaced by something I never thought I'd see in him. "I still have more bombs surrounding the property, and if you don't want to let my girl go..." *My girl.* I love the sound of that. "I'll make sure you guys return the rest of your pack in pieces."

Benji grabs me, and I go straight to him, hugging him and inhaling him deeply.

"We aren't giving her back," Samuel says. I'm surprised he speaks up for me to stay with him. I could have sworn I saw distaste in those coal eyes earlier. "She's ours to fuc..." Before he even finishes that sentence, Az grabs him by the neck and dismembers his head from his body. Blood splatters all over his face, and all I can do is stare with my mouth hanging wide open.

Shit, Az is fucking crazy. It surprised me that the bulky guy was still trying to get me back despite the contempt in his eyes, but I'm even more shocked when Az defends me. "Anybody else?" He looks at the other three Alpha men that are left. When he's satisfied with their horrified reaction, he continues. "She will stay with us and anyone who wants to get her will have to go through us first." Damn he sounds possessive too. I just didn't get that vibe from him when we talked the first time. I thought he truly wanted me to leave.

An object with a blinking red light catches my attention, and I see a camera in one of the trees. There's no doubt that Tyler is watching everything that's going on. He probably told the guys where I was at all times. That's how Ash was so confident that nothing was going to happen to me.

The men and the remnants of their crew start walking away toward their cars. "This isn't over. I'll be back for Kat. She's mine," Dan promises.

I narrow my eyes on him. "Never." I say softly. Dan keeps his eyes on me and I hold onto his stare angrily.

Benji turns me around so that I can't look at him. When I hear the car engines, I gasp. "My kids. I don't know where they are." I struggle in Benji's embrace, scared that Dan will hurt them if he can't have me. "We have to find them."

"You see that van over there?" Benji motions to a van that I wouldn't have noticed without him pointing it out to me. I look up at him and nod. "Tyler is in there with his equipment, and he has Ezra and Ava." Relief washes through my body. "You can't get rid of us that easily." He winks, and I'm not sure why, but my heart flutters with excitement.

CHAPTER 33

KAT

A sh is already making calls to have someone dispose of the bodies. I purposely look away from the gore of blood and dismembered limbs. My wolf side is another story, she doesn't mind all the bloodshed that streaks the green grass.

"Let's go see the kids." Benji grabs my shoulder and we walk to the van. My body tremors with the last of the adrenaline. I was so scared that I was going to die and leave them here. That's been twice this week, a bit too much for my comfort.

Tyler's huge grin greets me, and fuck if this guy isn't sexy with those pouty lips. It would make any woman's panties melt. "Kat, you can't stare at me like that when we've got kids around." He chuckles and I snap out of it before I see my kids.

"Mom!" My kid's shout, leaping out of the van to hug me. I notice that all the young boys that I met are here. Were they trying to keep an eye on my daughter? Is that why they're here? Or is it something more? I don't care either way. I'm just glad that she has good people in her life that are willing to protect her when I can't.

I look at Ezra and then Ava, my heart filling with sorrow. They've been through a lot these past couple of days. There have been more changes in our lives than I can possibly handle. I can't imagine the pain they're going through.

I watch as Ryder grabs her and pulls her into a hug, and she leans her head back in comfort.

As I look at Ash, pain crosses his features, and it seems like he wants to say something. He opens and closes his mouth rapidly like a fish out of water but nothing comes out. A bead of sweat runs down his forehead, and he wipes it away with a bloody arm.

Clearly aggravated, he stomps off, as if my presence alone has offended him.

Tight hands wrap around my shoulders, and just from the smell of pepper, amber wood, and citrus, I know that it's Benji. "Don't worry about him." He nuzzles my neck, inhaling deeply. "He's a grumpy old man." Ash growls but doesn't turn back around.

I glance around for Az, but he's nowhere to be found. No wait…he's staring at the bodies. What the fuck is… I don't get to think about it much longer when Benji drags me back into the white van.

The van is crowded with bodies but no one complains. We left Ash and Az behind to finish cleaning up the massacre. They'll probably have someone drive them home, although Az was acting strange, as if he were mesmerized by the blood.

When we get to the house, I remember something that Dan said to me, something that was life-altering to this pack.

My kids go up to their rooms with the rest of their friends. Tyler sprints past me to his room, computer in hand, and I can't help but wonder if he still has work to do.

I turn my concerned eyes to Benji. "What's up, Kitty Kat? You look like your brain is about to explode from thinking too hard." He chuckles but there's an edge to it. As if he's worried something might be wrong with me.

"There is something that Dan said that keeps nagging in the back of my mind." His body stills immediately, which makes me grow nervous.

"And what is that? His voice treads carefully." The sound of my erratic heartbeat matches his.

"He said that you guys are cur..." I don't get to finish that sentence because Benji's body drops to the floor, his body convulsing.

My mouth drops in shock, and I immediately run to him. His mouth is foaming as tears stream down my face. "Tyler help!" I yell.

He comes running down the stairs at full speed and crouches on the opposite side of me.

Benji's body stops shaking. "Is he dead?"

Tyler looks at me with haunted eyes and my stomach drops. This can't be good.

Acknowledgments

Thank you to my beta team Brenda, Faith, Karlie, Michelle, Nattiee and Oriane for reading my book and giving me all the suggestions. I appreciate you ladies so much.

Thank you Heather for helping me out. You're a badass working with a newborn and taking on my book! I admire you so much!

Thank you Hope Brown for creating beautiful graphics and games, helping me with my group, giveaways, and everything you do for me. I really appreciate your time and I'm grateful to have you in my author journey.

Thank you to my husband and my kids. I wouldn't have been able to follow through without them. My husband for believing in me and knowing that this is the path that I'm meant to be on. For reminding me that this is exactly what I want to do even when I get sidetracked and try to work on other stuff. My kids for watching put hours and hours into writing and being so patient, well, as patient as they could be. I love you guys so much! I hope you see that mommy is following her dreams and I hope it gives you the motivation to follow your own.

Last but not least to my readers. I can't thank you enough for picking this book and reading it. I hope you enjoyed reading my baby book and got lost in the world of Kat and her men. I can't wait to bring you the next book in the series. Thank you all for giving this book a chance from the bottom of my heart thank you!

ABOUT ANGELICA AQUILES

Angelica Aquiles lives in WA state with her two sons, her husband, and her dog. She goes out fishing, hiking, and now offroading with her family. When she has downtime she loves to get lost in a good book.

Join her FB Group:
https://www.facebook.com/groups/1107819209697422

[Instagram] instagram.com/angelicaaquilesauthor
[goodreads] goodreads.com/angelicaaquilesauthor
[amazon] amazon.com/~/e/B091QFG3Y2
[BB] bookbub.com/authors/angelica-aquiles

ALSO BY ANGELICA AQUILES

IRON BEAST PACK

Marked Wolf

Cursed Wolf

Alphas' Origins

Chosen Wolf

The Dark Sea (Little Mermaid Retelling)

Made in the USA
Columbia, SC
08 January 2023

74871551R00155